CAPTAIN STEEL and Other Stories
By Darin Wagner

"It's time to heave the lines and dodge the mines, big daddy." – old submariner apothegm

CAPTAIN STEEL
A novella by Darin Wagner

I'm going to tell you where it all started. Where it *really* came from.

What you are now reading is my account of what the President called "the greatest enormity of the 21st century." It will begin with a rather brief retrospective of two little boys who loved comic books and from there show how it relates to the "enormity" that we've all experienced. There is no way of telling you, fair reader, of the Biggest Damned Thing Since the Great Flood without telling our own little story first.

Mine and Timmy's, that is.

You're by now familiar with the 1.3 billion global death toll, the worldwide economic chaos and the loss of nearly all the great monuments celebrating man's achievements. Everybody left knows somebody who was killed in the terrible, swift onslaught. No new cars are going to be coming out for a while. Space shuttle launches are, for now, a thing of the past. Gone are the Statue of Liberty, the Great Wall of China, the Pyramids of Egypt and the Empire State Building, among many others. (All we've got left, it seems, are things like that huge twine ball in Hokah, Minnesota.)

When we get TV (as-we-*knew*-it) back, you will be exposed to accounts of how the "enormity" came about and how it was dealt with. You'll read books by historians on the subject and magazine interviews containing the memoirs of the survivors. Those accounts, however, will be told by persons who were not a part of what went down... not at the end, especially... an end which just took place not more than two hours ago. (I'm currently about 200 feet beneath Arctic ice heading south. My chauffeurs are the crew of the submarine USS *Sand Lance*.) When we get back "home" and the doctors confirm that I haven't got accelerated leukemia, I'll come back to this laptop and write the full-blown, unabridged book. For now though, you get the short version, just in case "the rest of my life" turns out to be a fugacious affair.

I.

My name is John Boyle and I'm an associate professor at the University of Wisconsin – Madison.

Up until a few days ago, I was also a comic book writer/artist whose past credits include *The Hellacious Hex-Men*, *Blue Bombardier*, *Pronto*, *Wonder Witch* and most recently of course, *Captain Steel*. My love of comic books started at the tender age of four-and-a-half. Like all kids since the mid-fifties, I participated in that ritualistic weekend morning ceremony of worship. I'm not talking about church on Sunday (although I had indeed gone to church until my late teens). No, I'm talking about the ritual that started with the Baby Boomers; cartoons on Saturday morning. "Challenge of The Superfriends" and "Herculoids" were among my favorites. Us kids would get up extra early on a day when most over the age of 17 were trying to sleep in, just to watch the animated programing that was neatly tucked in between each relentless sales pitch. (Said sales pitches directed exclusively toward those persons in society who didn't have jobs and, therefore, didn't have the money to buy what was being glorified before them. It was insidious, really; an entire corporate campaign designed to take advantage of the growing number of spoiled children in America, who were never more than a whine away from getting that rejected military suspension spring re-christened "The Slinky" or that box of Cap'n Crunch with the glow-in-the-dark pirate figurine at the bottom.) Every kid watched cartoons. Then one Friday night my dad and I stayed up and watched the premiere of a live-action show on CBS called "The Incredible Hulk." And there, before my young eyes, was a cartoon character who was *real* and not a moving two-dimensional illustration. I remember that realism and how it scared the living shit outta me the first time Bill Bixby flashed his white contact lenses and started ripping his clothes. I ran and hid behind the couch and, from that secure locale, watched Lou Ferrigno snarl and toss crooks around. This anxiety became a common thing for me while simultaneously enjoying the show. My mother could see that, even though I was fascinated by the title character, he was perhaps a little too intense for my four-and-a-half-year-old psyche to endure. So in an attempt to put me at ease, she went out and bought me a comic book featuring the "Ol' Greenskin." Her hope was that it would take the edge off of the terror that the show induced in me. It worked, but it also had two unforeseen side-effects:

     A.) I learned to read faster than the average kid, which Mom liked.

B.) I became hooked on comic books and started what would eventually become a rather large collection of them. That latter side effect has chafed Mom's sanity ever since. My eventual employment and success in the business of creating comic books only slightly altered my mother's opinion of the medium, which is still in the resounding negative.

(On that "learning to read faster" part, all I can say is that reading "Hulk smash! Hulk smash puny humans!!!" was a Hell of a lot more exciting than reading "See Dick. See Dick run.")

But that's enough about me for right now.

II.

Gale, Wisconsin was the town where I lived as a boy. Of the 3,704 citizens who populated that miserably dull speck on the countryside, the only other kid my age who read comic books like I did was Timmy Shimmerhorn. We met and became friends while in the first grade. I had just moved to town that fall and Timmy and I were unaware of our mutual interest until Halloween, when we came to school dressed up for the costume party. He was Captain Steel and I was the Hulk.

The bond was immediate.

Timmy and I shared many an afternoon afterward playing like little boys often do... sometimes using action figures and sometimes squirt-guns. (This was back before the Super-Soaker, when squirt-guns were just clear plastic pistols that had a range of maybe five feet if you were lucky.) We also sat and daydreamed together, usually about comics and the characters featured in them. Questions that we commonly debated were ones like "How *exactly* does Spider-Man crawl up walls?" and "Can Green Lantern's power ring actually create something that is yellow?" These were deep intellectual conversations in logic and observation for our grade-school minds. We were the only two in town who were knowledgeable enough to butt heads on these subjects. Sometimes we'd get into such discussions on the school playground and the other kids, most of whom were more interested in sports and cars, would attempt to take sides. All of the kids watched cartoons on Saturday morning but when it came to superheroes, that was the extent of everybody else's knowledge. Timmy and I knew the "real" versions of the superheroes, the original versions printed in the original medium from which all other superhero-featuring media were derived.

Once, while we were at the local swimming pool, Timmy got into an accident in which some girl trying to do a doggie paddle ended up slashing his lower lip with her nails. It was one of those cases where the two swimmers had their eyes closed underwater and it was as close to dying as Timmy had come thus far in his life. The blood terrified him. I remember carrying his thin little body into the school looking for the nurse while he wailed and sobbed because the lifeguard on duty had done nothing about it except kick us out of the pool. The lifeguard was the older sister of the girl who had clawed him and did nothing to console Timmy as the deep gash in his lip let blood out in surges. When I found the nurse, who was there on the off chance doing paperwork that Saturday, she took us to the local clinic and arranged for the school district to pay for Timmy's stitches.

As fate would have it, Timmy got the chance to repay me for the swimming pool incident later that winter when we were ambushed by older junior high kids and their arsenal of snow balls. One of their projectiles turned out to be more of an ice ball than a snow ball and struck me in the eye. Hard. After I "came to" a few minutes later, Timmy had to guide me home because I couldn't see or walk all that well. He also helped identify the kids who had knocked me out and given me my swollen shiner.

I was the only boy he had for a friend back then. A couple of the little girls in our class were friends with him in early grade school, probably because he shared very few interests with other boys. Timmy was polite and courteous, something which most boys were/are not. It was almost an enemy-of-my-enemy sort of thing. He'd sit with the girls at lunch from time-to-time and gab with them. It was like a munchkin sewing circle. Gradually, however, Timmy came to sit with me more and more at lunch.

We were a match, him and I. Our camaraderie was seemingly without equal among our peers. He and I were the best of friends and we stayed that way until age 12.

That was when I started noticing some things about Timmy that weren't quite right.

III.

Timmy was my height, but he weighed much less than I. This was due to a couple of factors: The first was his low level of physical activity. He and I were not into sports, so we weren't in as good a shape as most of the other kids. (I was a little overweight while he was drastically underweight.) About the only exercise Timmy usually got was riding his bike with me to go get comics once a month. I taught him how to ride his bike. Eventually, however, his mother decided that it would be better if she got his comics for him on her way home from work.

The second factor contributing to Timmy's lack of mass was malnutrition. His father had been an alcoholic and ran off with some other woman years earlier, leaving Timmy and his mother, a paramedic at the time, to fend for themselves. Now, one would think that with a nurse for a mother Timmy would have been healthier, but this was not the case. Timmy's typical breakfast was a can of Mountain Dew and a small dish of Fritos. He didn't eat cereal because he didn't like milk. He said it tasted sour. This was another little quirk of Timmy's; if something didn't agree with him once, he would never give it another chance. Apparently, he once drank some sour milk. Hence, milk was sour. He could not be convinced otherwise, no matter how hard I tried. He was the same way with fish. His mother cooked fish sticks for him for dinner once and gave them to him while they were still too hot. He ended up burning his tongue. In Timmy-logic, this meant that *all* fish burned his tongue and, therefore, he was unwilling to eat fish ever again. When you tried to tell him that no edible fish at the store would burn someone's tongue unless it was ingested too soon after being cooked, Timmy would insist that it had nothing at all to do with temperature. He'd say that his tongue was super-sensitive and that enzymes or something in the fish (which normal tongues were incapable of detecting) hurt his taste buds. Then he'd get upset and start pouting because you challenged his delusion. I'm not making this up. In the spirit of detente, I learned to avoid this subject with him. Timmy's mom also never contested his ever twisting eating habits either. At school, the bagged lunches she sent with him typically consisted of a peanut butter and jelly sandwich, an apple and some sort of Hostess treat, usually a Sno-ball. He would virtually inhale the Sno-ball, take two bites out of the sandwich and toss the rest of the sandwich along with the untouched apple into the trash. That was how Timmy ate.

Timmy also watched too much TV. Now, it can be argued that most kids watch too much TV, but with Timmy it was blatantly obvious. When we had first met, cable television hadn't yet reached Gale. Saturday morning cartoons were just an appetizer after cable came. When it did arrive, Timmy usually watched it down in his basement all day long unless we got together to play or unless he was reading a comic book. Coaxing him out of that dark, dank hole was often hard to do and sometimes I lost those battles. But, getting back to the whole "too much tv thing": Timmy had built up, through years of substituting TV for real life experiences and human interaction, a template for behavior which mimicked that which he saw. On television, people overreact. This is especially true of situation comedies. In sitcoms, like "Three's Company" or "Seinfeld," the smallest little thing is blown drastically out of proportion by the characters in order to earn the audible cheers from that unseen, and oft times absent-altogether, studio audience. (Watch one and specifically look for this, once America gets all of its precious TV networks back, if it ever does.) Watch an old "Perfect Strangers" episode and try to hypothetically apply those mannerisms to your home or workplace. Trust me. You'll get the idea.

Timmy overreacted to everything. Little example: Once I called his house during the day. He answered the phone and, when he found out it was me, he immediately started chastising me, saying, "Don't you know my mother is sleeping!?" Timmy's mother had just started working the graveyard shift, you see. In retrospect, I think he knew somewhere in the back of his mind that it was ridiculous to assume that I would know something like that... but he didn't care as long as he got to have his dramatic, self-satisfying moment. He looked for drama everywhere. The problem was that his "life" wasn't very exciting and didn't offer much material for him to work with or react to. So he reacted dramatically to as many little things that came along as he could. It became a rather annoying, later *disturbing*, idiosyncrasy of his. Timmy was the star of his own little sitcom... but the canned laughter, however, was only for him to hear.

Before one reaches puberty, one can get by with taking a single bath or shower per week. Timmy never adjusted his bathing habits as we grew toward our teens. I remember one time in junior high our Math teacher, Mr. Elgin, patted Timmy on the head after he answered a remedial math problem correctly. (Timmy was terrible at math problems because he always guessed the answers rather than trying to actually *solve* for them.) Elgin suddenly pulled his hand away from Timmy's head in disgust and started rubbing said hand on his pants. "Dammit boy! Don't you ever SHOWER?!" yelled Elgin. Timmy's hair was usually so full of natural lanolin that it behaved almost like freshly gelled hair.

Timmy's wardrobe was a couple years behind him, too. He always wore high-water pants, mismatched socks and no belt. Once during junior high, our class went to the swimming pool for Phy-Ed. (Oh by the way, in keeping with his aforementioned philosophy, Timmy was never willing to go back to the swimming pool after that day in the clinic with the gashed lip. He had protested dramatically to the Phy-Ed teacher, who also happened to be the football coach. The Phy-Ed teacher, who never gave Timmy much thought up until that point, asked why Timmy should not muster with the rest of the kids at the pool. Timmy said "because." The towering Phy-Ed teacher, looking as though he was smelling onions, then asked "because *why*?" and Timmy said "because I hate the pool." The Phy-Ed teacher told Timmy to "fulfill his gender role" and Timmy ended up at the pool anyway.) While I was changing into my trunks, I heard the snickers and laughs of the other guys. I looked up and saw that they were all pointing at Timmy in his Captain Steel underwear. His mother had bought those for him years earlier at a rummage sale. They fit him like speedos at this point. As the boys all laughed, Timmy's face glared back at them with a grim configuration reminiscent of Judge Dredd or the Punisher. But that only made the boys laugh harder.

Nobody ever took him seriously because he always went so ridiculously over-the-top.

By high school, the two of us had drifted completely apart. No, that's not right. *I* drifted from *him*. Everybody did, even the munchkin sewing circle. Timmy, you see, had what I call "Peter Pan Syndrome." He never grew up. (No, I'm not a psychologist, so feel free to reject my opinion if this is your field.) When you talked to Timmy, it was just like talking to him a few years earlier because his speech pattern hadn't changed much past the fifth grade. Intellectually, he was stunted. While the rest of us were reading novels from the likes of Michael Crichton and Kim Stanley Robinson, Timmy could be found thoroughly enthralled by the latest Dragonlance paperback (all of which are written in a third-grade reading level) or a Choose-Your-Own-Epic book. (Of the latter, The Cavern of Time and Driftwood City were the ones I saw him reading in high school. I remembered both of these books as having already been read to us in the second and third grade by our homeroom teachers. He didn't read any that hadn't already been read to him because that would have been too much work.)

Years of not eating right had also taken their toll on him. He had the build of an Auschwitz survivor and his head was too narrow. As his baby teeth had fallen out and been replaced by the larger adult teeth, his skull and jaw refused to expand to accommodate them. This left him with a mouth full of jumbled teeth that grew in all directions.

I was still reading comic books, sure, but I was also into other things by high school. Said things included *real* books, the school newspaper, mock trial and even exercise. I would pass him in the halls and, when he invariably made eye contact with me, I'd nod. He would hold his head high and very astutely reply "John" back to me, like he was Alfred the Butler or some other ultra-proper character. I pitied the poor guy, but there was not much, if anything, I could do for him. He was a misfit and he seemed pretty content with that, mostly. I think he resented his status, but was too hopelessly lost in his own habits and acedia to change. He thought the rest of us should change instead.

He was smart in some areas, but he seldom displayed this in school. This was because his ambitions were reserved for only those subjects that he was interested in. Besides comic books, he also seemed to be interested in the sword and sorcery genre and in his ColecoVision (later, Nintendo). Pretty much every summer since third grade, he ended up having to go to summer school. At first he thought it was the end of the world. By high school, he had accepted it and became complacent with his own academic underachievement.

I tried to talk with him once during our junior year. We were in the school library and I came over and sat at his table, across from him. (No one liked to sit near him because he usually smelled like pee.) I asked him how things were going.

He immediately shouted, "I can't believe they did that to THOR!!"

I looked around to see if other students were watching us.

They were.

I turned back to Timmy and asked, "Who?"

"THE AVENGERS!! Who do you THINK?!" was what he yelled back.

I was also reading *The Mighty Avengers* at that time and knew what he was talking about. (The writer of the comic, a great guy and later friend of mine, had changed the Avengers roster and had cut the Thor character from it in order to better accommodate the writer of the regular *Thor* title.) I looked into Timmy's eyes and saw an intensity there. It was a look that I'll remember when I'm old and grey, if I make it. I knew that he knew Thor and the Avengers were not real, but his eyes made me question this. This was dramatic, even for him. His attitude suggested to me that perhaps he cared about these characters just a bit too much. I never really talked about the comics I read anymore, at least not in the school library. I usually saved that kind of conversation for the owner of Sarge's Cards & Comics in nearby Tomah... but even then, I didn't talk about the characters the way *he* was talking about the characters. He proceeded to tell me how happy he was for Les Lincoln (a.k.a. Captain Steel), who had married Tenille Trust, the Captain's girlfriend since 1938. He also mentioned how much he disliked Iron Man's new armor. He said the new Robin was useless and that Batman should get rid of him and bring back Dick Grayson. Then he went on to tell me how he *loved* Zatanna's fishnet stockings and how much he wanted to marry someone like her or Wonder Girl. (While I was using *Playboy* and *Penthouse*, Timmy was apparently using *Teen Titans*.) The conversation reminded me of the last time I talked with Grampa Boyle before Alzheimers finally took him. Timmy was talking about these characters as if they were real people. Some of whom he had been talking to just prior to my sitting down at his table, by the sound of him. That was the last time I talked with Timmy Shimmerhorn.

Timmy barely graduated high school. Our class had a 100% graduation rate and I've always suspected that he was pushed through for "political" reasons. When I left Gale, I had my driver's license. Timmy did not have his and I assumed he never would.

I was right.

My feet and hands are starting to get numb and prickly at the same time. It's probably nothing, but just in case it isn't I'll pick up the pace a bit.

IV.

For me, things went fairly well after high school. I went to UW-Madison and got my BA and MA in English while simultaneously selling a couple of short stories to magazines like *Weird Yarns* and *Cool Stories*. I even got a story called "Vanishing Cream" published in *Playboy*. Then, while at the Chicago Comicon one year, I met the editor from Republic Comics. She had read my work in sci-fi prose and wanted to know if I'd consider writing for them. I gave her a proposal for one of their lesser titles that wasn't selling well. She liked it and I got the gig. Apparently I was doing something very, very right because said title (*Pronto*) went from being in danger of cancellation to being a top seller with rave reviews pretty much overnight. I've been writing (and occasionally editing) comics ever since. On the side I've also managed to publish four novels, all crime noir. The last two made the New York Times Best Seller List's top ten and there were negotiations in the works for a film based on one or more of the books. Things were going very well. I was now getting paid very well for my daydreaming.

Eventually, I hooked the comic book project of a lifetime; I became the writer of one of the Captain Steel titles, specifically *Captain Steel: Man of Marvels*. (The other three Captain Steel titles were *Captain Steel*, *The Adventures of Captain Steel* and *Excellent Comics starring Captain Steel*.)

Captain Steel. The first superhero.

Now, I don't see any point in spending too much of your time describing Captain Steel to you, hypothetical reader. Everybody knows who he is, especially *now*. Some of my intellectual brethren in the English department always argued that superheroes existed in fiction far earlier than Captain Steel's debut. They often liked to cite Heracles. I, however, maintain that the specific combination of superpowers (or skills), a secret identity, tights, an urban setting and the very designation "superhero," make the genre a uniquely American creation. Too many of my colleagues are so totally against anything good being prescribed to America that it really gets pathetic sometimes.

To save myself some time, here is the article I did for *The Pacific Monthly* a few of years ago, when the Captain was celebrating another of his career milestones:

He's 60!
The granddaddy of all superheroes reaches a milestone, always evolving but still impervious
Guest Article by John Boyle

> *Behold, I teach you the overman. The overman is the meaning of the earth.*
> - Friedrich Nietzche

> *"I was sitting in the bath one day when I had a goofy idea. I envisioned an earth-bound god, or demi-god who was an amalgamation of Achilles, Heracles, Abraham Lincoln and all the legendary characters of old that I could think of. And that was just the beginning."*
> - Terrance Stiller

Swifter than a streaking rocket!
More awesome than a fighting battleship!
Able to endure the molten heat of raging volcano!
Behold, Captain Steel!
That's right, kids... Captain Steel!
Whose might can tame the most violent of storms,
Rend a tank to scrap metal,
And who, disguised as...

We've all heard this before right? Of course we have. It's scripture. It's ingrained into our culture and etched into our memories as surely as the Pledge of Allegiance is. Captain Steel set the standard for an entire sub-genre of fantasy. He and his supporting cast are household words/names and there isn't one American who hasn't enjoyed an adventure or two starring the good Captain, whether it is one contained in his native comic books, his radio shows of old, or his numerous screen appearances, both small and silver. The Captain is the third most recognizable fictitious character worldwide, his familiarity surpassed only by Mickey Mouse and Bugs Bunny.

Where do such enduring legends come from? Where do mythological titans come from? What makes Captain Steel such an integral and enduring part of pop culture Americana? "I had always kinda wanted to be that guy everybody looked up to, but I was also pretty thankful that I wasn't. I thought, 'What if a guy could have both? What if a guy could be Heracles, but never let it go to his head and also led an ordinary life on the side? What kind of man could do that?'"

A single epiphany, or even a collection of small ones that seem to emerge all at the same time, ascend from a underlying bed of personal experiences. Terry Stiller was a skinny, four-eyed teen who drifted through his high school in Monmouth County, New Jersey. His paper route garnered him a mere $3.75 per week and most of that contributed to the greater good of the family. He saved a fraction of his meager earnings for the adventures of Captain Buck Rodgers, Sherlock

Holmes and Flash Gordon. Mimeographing his own versions of these pulp heroes, he circulated them amongst his classmates. A lesser epic of Stiller's, called *The Reign of Captain Steel*, spotlighted a clumsy dictator from the future wearing a kaiser helmet. It wasn't the stuff of greatness, but it was the start of something grand. After a hard day at his new job at a local steel mill, months after Stiller had graduated, that grand thing finally came to him: Drop the helmet and make Captain Steel a hero. Hard to believe the character started out as comic relief, but then, there was a time when Mickey Mouse was a rabbit. Terry Stiller's good friend, the late Paul Random, helped refine the costume and overall design of the character. The two had been friends since childhood and continued to write and draw their character's adventures for years, even after fledgling id Comics bought the rights from them in 1941.

Today, of course, Captain Steel is an American institution. After more than a half-century of heroic antics in the pages of his native medium of comic books, 13 years of radio shows, 15 animated cartoons, three movie serials of ten installments each, two television series, more animated cartoons, a Broadway musical and five feature films and, not to mention, a plethora of products including T shirts, rings, sleeping bags, mugs and ball caps, the Captain has become a rather unique phenomenon.

"He is our American myth," says *Captain Steel: The Movie* screenwriter, Dan Oldman. "Some of my colleagues thought I was wasting my time with that one (the movie) and that I should have been concentrating on something more mature, like *The*

Godfather or *Apocalypse Now*-type films. I told them, 'No way man! This is an American icon we're talking about!'"

The Captain's publisher, id Comics, has rented out a part of Manhattan's Puck Building in order to throw a party of superheroic proportion; several thousand fans are expected to attend and watch video segments, buy merchandise and devour cake. Also this year, the Smithsonian opened a new exhibition, displaying Captain Steel memorabilia. The small town of Intrepid City, Montana, they have refurbished for summer tourists a large statue that boasts the rather erroneous declaration that this is "Captain Steel's hometown." In Monmouth County, New Jersey, which is the true hometown of the Captain, a booster club that calls itself the "Everlasting Battle" is planning an international Captain Steel event, complete with a ticker-tape parade.

Perhaps the thing that has contributed the most to Captain Steel's longevity and timeless appeal is that he continually undergoes superficial changes to fit the times, but never are his morals and values compromised. His costume has changed very little since his introduction, unlike the costumes and looks of other such heroes, like the Flash or Daredevil. His powers have increased exponentially since his first appearance, to the point where he seems nearly omnipotent. His fame has spread world-wide. And yet, through it all he remains a character bound by humility and morals. He refuses to accept himself as the titan that he is. Despite the fact that he has to face more temptation than anyone else, the Captain remains a public servant. (How many of us would be satisfied with that?) While this may be unrealistic, it still establishes a clear and indelible image to accompany that old axiom, "Just because you can do a thing, it does not necessarily mean that you should do said thing."

snip

That's enough of that article. The damn thing makes me sick now.

Captain Steel was Timmy's favorite superhero.

As kids, we both had the second movie memorized. "Captain Steel II" had been our favorite one in the series when we were kids because its plot pitted the title character against three similarly powered villains from outer space and it represented a high water mark in special effects at that time. Later in life, I came to appreciate the first film more than the second. "Captain Steel: The Movie," had brilliant cinematography, mythic overtones and stellar performances by Marlon Brando and Gene Hackman. The actor who played the Captain in this series of films was Reed Christopherson. He had always been, in my opinion, the perfect Captain Steel. He was exactly how I thought the Captain would look in real life.

I was very wrong about that.

V.

Timmy was not present at the five-year high school reunion. His absence went largely unnoticed by those in attendance. An old girlfriend of mine mentioned that she had heard that Timmy and his mother had moved to Milwaukee about a year after graduation, however.

VI.

At the ten-year reunion, Timmy was again a no-show. Nobody seemed to mind. In fact, several people cracked jokes about him and the way he behaved. One guy even suggested that he might be an acting coach for Pee Wee Herman. I must confess; I laughed.

VII.

Two years ago and not long after I had gotten the *Captain Steel* gig, I attended the Chicago Comicon much like I had been doing every year since I first broke into the industry. The line of people waiting to get a signed copy of *Captain Steel: Man of Marvels* #300 (which was a special double-sized issue) was the longest such line I'd ever had at a con. I was sharing the booth with Ross Caesar, who had painted a breathtaking cover for the issue. The cover was in keeping with Ross's distinctive style and was a dramatic reinterpretation of the cover of *Excellent Comics* #1. For those of you who were not comic book fans, *Excellent Comics* #1, published in 1938, contained the first appearance of Captain Steel and the cover featured the character tossing a Panzer into a wall covered with Nazi propaganda while the SS scattered in bewilderment. The Ross version of this image was fully painted and realistically depicted this same scene but from the angle and perspective of a spectator.

Towards the end of closing time, the line was still long. I had been signing copies of the issue for two days and had, for a while, grown pretty weary of it. It wasn't that my hand was getting fatigued or that I was tired of smiling. It was something else. The fans. Roughly half of the people who approached the table fit the stereotypical profile of the comic book fan; fat, pimply and smelly. Now, don't get me wrong; I *do* appreciate them and their admiration for my work. Oh, and the fact that they are also willing to part with $2.95-$3.75 plus tax for a brand new comic with my name on it and, sometimes, as much as $30 for an older comic with my name on it. My appreciation for that only goes so far, however. Most of those people ("fanboys," as they are known in the industry) should have soaked in betadine for at least a few hours before they came to see me. To steal part of a quote from Dennis Miller; each one smelled like a sweaty bum "eating Limburger cheese, while getting a permanent, in a septic tank, at a slaughterhouse."

My nose had lucked out for the last half-hour, though. This was because the primary demographic group in line towards the end of the con had been yuppie speculators. I don't like these guys. These are the guys who walk into a comic book store and buy up all of the #1 issues in the hopes that said issues will all go up in value by a factor of ten after two months' time. They're "investors." These guys don't read the comics. They appraise them. They don't appreciate their artistic value but they hope that others will. The only plus that this group has earned from me is that they are usually very well groomed and smell wonderful.

As I was signing a copy for one of these suits, I caught a whiff of something else. The smell was familiar and, for a split second, it reduced me to child of nine. The smell took me someplace. Someplace dark. A basement.

Timmy's basement.

I looked up and scanned what portion of the line that was visible. For a split second, my eyes caught a rather androgynous looking individual standing two or three people from the end of the line. "It's Timmy," my nose told me. "Bullshit," was what the rest of me, particularly my eyes, retorted. The person standing some 100 feet away from me was bizarre. At first glance, I thought it was an old woman, but in the two seconds of time which I spent looking at the figure, I realized that whomever it was might be either male or female. The hair was long and stringy and very obviously dyed slate grey. The skin was a sickly pale pallor that did nothing to hide the blue veins underneath. The thin lips appeared black. The figure was wearing a long black Navy raincoat and black jeans with black boots. The narrow head was cocked forward in my direction as if in concentration on me. The eyes of this-person-whose-smell-was-familiar appeared to be slightly rolled back, like a zombie.

And then the person was gone, as was the smell.

VIII.

Now is when the story starts to take on greater familiarity with you, patient reader. I came to be aware of it all at probably the same time most other

Americans did. Twenty years from now, virtually everyone's going to remember vividly where they were and what they were doing when they first heard the news on the radio or saw one of the many reports on television... much in the same way that the Baby Boomers all remember the JFK assassination or the people in my age group also remember the Challenger disaster.

It was, of course, Wednesday, March 10th of this year.

I had just come home from the local mall with my brand new copy of "Dirty Harry: The Special Edition." As is usual for me anytime I come home with a new video, I immediately went to my living room set-up, booted it up and started playing the disc. Headline News is what I had left the set on the night before. (I came home late from a figure drawing session at the University and I wanted to catch the results of the Hitmen vs Outlaws game.) As the TV screen came to life, I caught a glimpse of something familiar on the screen right before the DVD player overrode the cable signal with the movie's FBI warning. I fumbled for the DVD remote and hit "STOP."

That familiar thing was the logo of the Captain Steel comics and it was floating next to the head of a female news anchor. I don't have a photographic memory, but this is how I remember the anchor's report. It went like this:

"Again the breaking story this hour: thousands of Americans have made statements this morning, claiming to have seen a flying man. The reports have come from four major cities coast-to-coast so far and common among them all is description of the man's attire, which bares a striking resemblance to that of cartoon character Captain Steel."

It's a joke, I thought. *A Hoax. Has to be.* I immediately began to recall a notorious skyscraper climber in New York years ago who dressed up in a red and blue suit and called himself "Spider-Dan." But the newscaster had said "thousands of Americans" had seen this thing. Not only seen it, but had gone *on record* as having seen it. *UFO sightings usually don't get that kind of turn out,* I thought.

The news anchor then turned the story over to a correspondent. The man with the microphone was standing in the middle of Times Square.

"At approximately 8 a.m. this morning hundreds of New Yorkers here in Manhattan claim to have witnessed someone or something flying unaided through the city at high speed. More than half of the those we've talked to told us that the flyer's attire matched that of comic strip superhero Captain Steel."

The screen then shifted to an old woman standing on a sidewalk with microphones being held in front of her by persons off camera. "Helen Wolcott, who works at the Pierre in Manhattan, said she saw it as she was about to enter the housekeepers' entrance and clock in for the day."

"As I was at the door swiping my key card, I heard a 'whoosh' sound and a lot of commotion. So I turned around and saw a shadow moving across the street. When I looked up, I saw a man sorta hovering about a block away and, God, he must have been about three stories up in the air. Then he started moving again and went right over my head. Whoever he was, he was wearing a dark blue suit with a small red cape," said the Wolcott woman.

The correspondent continued, "Then, approximately fifteen minutes later, nearly the same thing happened in Chicago, followed by Denver ten minutes after that and twenty minutes later, Los Angeles. Witnesses continue to come forward at this hour claiming to have spotted the officially unidentified flying object in other parts of the country as well."

The broadcast switched back to the news room and the anchor.

"We'll keep you posted on this story as it develops twice an hour. For more information, be sure to tune into CNN for co-"

I flipped to CNN.

They were running last night's Harry Ling Live. *Obviously, the situation couldn't be that major if they aren't preempting a re-run*, I thought. I figured the whole thing was bullshit and that Headline News must have been hurting for copy again. (I once saw them do a story on a man who had buried his dog's puppies alive in his back yard and how his dog had "heroically" dug them back up. Not exactly a headline, if you ask me.) I continued to play my new disc.

When the movie was over and I'd seen all of the special features on the disc, I stopped the player and immediately became a deer in headlights.

On the screen was a still photo image of a blur that could only have been the flying man from Headline News. The anchor mentioned how the subject of the photo was seen "levitating at high speed" above and through the cities of New York, Chicago, Denver and Los Angeles. The number of sightings now reported had reached the millions. In the back of my head, I did some quick mental math; the first sighting had been at around 8 a.m. in New York and the one in Los Angeles had been, according to new and more accurate information, about an hour later. *So unless this is more than one guy*, I thought, *he can make a cross-country flight in about an hour*.

It was after watching two more hours of this live coverage that I got a call from Rick Quedilla, my *Captain Steel* editor over at the id Comics offices in New York. He sounded rather excited. Watching the news reports and listening to him simultaneously was a challenge, but I did get the impression that Rick thought the situation was pretty damn cool. He kept mentioning public interest increases and corresponding sales increases. I interrupted him by asking if this was some kind of elaborate gimmick that the folks at the id offices had cooked up. He said, "Not no, but Hell no!"

I then asked him, "Then who's responsible?"

Rick was silent for a few seconds, then he said, "*I* dunno! That's the legal department's job!"

"Aren't you curious about this, Rick?" I asked him.

"Well, yeah..." he grudgingly replied.

"I mean, this whatever-it-is has apparently been zooming all over the country this morning. He's gone from New York to LA twice now and, according to the news, satellite surveillance indicates he's swinging back around for another lap. Why?"

"Look, this is very fascinating, don't get me wrong, but I can't help but see this as golden, John. Think about it. The *Captain Steel* titles are going to be sought after by every Tom, Dick and Annie, every Kookla, Fran and Ollie and every Moe, Larry and Curly in the fuckin' world. This is big, John. This is pretty fuckin' big. We're millionaires. You do realize that, right?"

"I don't like it," I said flatly while looking at CNN's latest computer-generated map of the country. This one had on it all the cities that had been visited marked with an animated (spinning) version of Captain Steel's "S" icon.

"What?!" Rick asked, surprised.

As I was about to repeat myself, there was a loud but very distant cracking sound outside. It sounded like thunder or a jet making a sonic boom. It only distracted me for a second. "I said 'I don't like it.' Let me ask you something, Rick. If Captain Steel were a real guy and not just a comic book character, what would he be doing right now?"

There was silence on the line. Then Rick spoke up. "Saving lives? Helping people?"

"Exactly," I told him. "But he *hasn't*. All he's been doing is making brief appearances in major cities. He makes sure people see him, then he takes off for the next city at high speed, then he swings back around and does it all over again. So, there are two possibilities. Either this is a hoax for publicity, and for the life of me I can't figure out how they could pull all this off if it were... Or..."

I hesitated in order to find the words.

"Or?" Rick beckoned.

"Or we've got some kind of freak flying around at Mach 3 dressed up like our favorite good guy."

Rick didn't know what to say about that.

I continued. "It's like he doesn't know what to do, or maybe what he *can* do. If we assume that before today, whoever this is couldn't fly or simply wasn't around, then I would say he's gauging his abilities... getting familiar with them. Hold on, Rick..."

The news coverage had just put an alert graphic on the screen. They cut to the team of assembled news anchors who were now covering the phenomenon in the studio. The one in the middle, the senior among them, made the announcement. "Several hundred miles of the heartland have been devastated within the past few minutes, apparently due to an intense shockwave that appears to have taken place along the UFO's flight path between the Quad Cities and Philadelphia. The figures are just starting to come in, but preliminary data from satellite would seem to indicate that the shockwave has destroyed thousands of acres of populated areas. However, unpopulated areas appear to be untouched."

"Did you hear that Rick?"I asked.

Rick wasn't listening. I could hear commotion and excitement over the phone in the background.

"Rick?"

More commotion.

"Rick?!"

I could hear a woman in the background shout with excitement, "He's here! Look!"

Even more commotion.

Finally, Rick was on the phone again. "He's here, man! Can you believe this shit? He's right in front of the building, about two floors up and on the other side of the street!"

"Rick, get out of the office. You need to get away from him," I told him with a calm 911 voice.

"Geez man, his shoulders are huge! He's bigger'n Arnold *ever* was!"

"Rick, get yourself and everybody else out of there. Now!"

"Hey, his eyes are..."

"RICK! EVERY TOWN IN HIS FLIGHT PATH BETWEEN IOWA AND PENNSYLVANIA IS GONE! HE FLEW OVER THEM TOO FAST, BUT HE DIDN'T SPEED UP UNTIL HE CAME TO EACH ONE!!"

The phone went dead before I could finish the part about "too fast."

I turned back to my big screen tv. About three minutes later, CNN had something new to report. They showed live footage of the destruction of the Busiek Building, which, among other things, contained the corporate headquarters and offices of id Comics. The unstable footage, obviously shot by someone in a nearby building, showed a tiny human form hovering among the massive office buildings of New York. The figure was just hovering. One could see people gathering at the windows on his side of the building. A second later, the building collapsed, as though being demolished with dynamite, with what must have been almost a thousand souls trapped inside. As it fell, the figure never budged.

I sat and watched them repeat that footage over and over for the next twenty minutes or so. When they played it in slow motion, I saw why the building had collapsed. For a split second, two green lines had flashed between the blurry-but-stationary form of "Captain Steel" and the place where the building met the concrete floor of the city. The two lines briefly traced the foundation of the building and then abruptly vanished. I'm not in the habit of talking to myself, but after watching the scene for a third time, my dumbfounded brain finally comprehended and came upon a realization.

"He's got laservision," I whispered under my breath. I put my head in my hands and listened to the footage. Eventually, I lifted my eyes back to the screen.

The carnage belonged in the Old Testament.

IX.

After New York, the media had unanimously began calling the mysterious visitor "Captain Steel." It was fitting since he not only apparently looked the part, but also displayed the various physical qualities that the role required. A combination of satellite surveillance footage (which was surprisingly clear and crisp) and news helicopter footage chronicled the speedy fall of the Big Apple. All of us have seen the nightmare images. Captain Steel destroyed every building in Manhattan in just under 10 minutes. People in the streets fleeing the city were microwaved as he attenuated his laservision to a wide aperture and bathed them in the searing heat of his gaze. They caught fire and continued to run until they *popped*. Others had their bodily fluids crystalized by Captain Steel's breath as he used it to encase them in transparent glaciers. He toppled some of the buildings by flying up to them and punching through their supports. Several times he would already begin attacking one building before the last one had completely fallen to the streets. It rained concrete. Captain Steel never walked; he stayed airborne the entire time, sometimes merely a few feet off of the ground. We never really got a look at him because he was moving too fast for the cameras. They couldn't keep him centered. He used his breath to freeze the Chrysler Building until its then-brittle frame couldn't maintain its own weight nor the additional weight of the tons upon tons of ice that had formed on it. The Man Of Marvels looked at the Statue of Liberty and the liquified copper from the statue flowed like lava over Liberty Island and into the river. Central Park erupted in a near-nuclear mushroom of fire. The Brooklyn Bridge was falling down like its London cousin in that nursery rhyme. The MetLife Building became MetDeath Building and then ceased to be a building at all. A few of New York's finest surrounded the Captain, pulled out their sidearms and wasted their bullets before being crushed by falling debris. The Captain's actions seemed deliberate and strategic at first but, half way through the process of removing the city from the face of the Earth, he seemed to become more nonchalant. His movements became leisurely, it seemed. Then he turned his attention to the things that were buzzing around in the air and that's when the helicopter stopped relaying images and sound to Atlanta.

He did much the same thing to Chicago, then Los Angeles. (You could hear what was going on in Chicago all the way to Madison, 140 miles away.) This all happened between 8 a.m. and 2 p.m.. When he arrived in L.A., the Air Force was waiting for him. It was a thorough exercise in futility and really quite a waste. I could go into it more, but I wouldn't be telling you anything you don't already know.

After Captain Steel had finished L.A., the President gave a State of the Union address, via satellite, to the what remained of the nation. That speech was cut short by the destruction of Washington D.C. before the President had managed to get to the point.

Captain Steel then headed for Europe.

X.

So transfixed was I on the disasters that were befalling the world that everyday concerns fell into the foggy depths of my subconscious. Perhaps it was shock and the realization that I was in shock that prompted me to desperately dive into that fog, digging through it, trying to recapture normalcy. I needed something normal. Mundane. Ordinary. Something. I needed to check my mail. In the 90 minutes it took for the Captain to traverse the Atlantic, I remembered this comparatively minor domestic regularity and trotted out to the end of my driveway. It was good to get even that far away from the television. Across the street, the Stamfords were vigorously packing their Explorer. Packing it with the intent of not coming back, no doubt. Mrs. Stamford paused for a moment and just looked at me. Then she shrieked and started lobbing things at me with surprising accuracy. "My mother" and "Chicago" were the only things I could make out in between her sobbing hysterics. She was upset, but she didn't traverse the street and confront me up close. (She had always been like that. She would never come over and tell the neighbors that they were being too loud herself. She always called the police and then watched the situation from her living room window.) Mr. Stamford came out of the house and got her into their vehicle. As they left, he gave me a look that plainly said I was guilty by association. The rest of the neighborhood appeared to be normal, calm and serene. I guess the reality of the situation hadn't really sank in with everybody yet. Who could blame them?

The previous day's mail was still in the box and it was mostly the usual sort of trash that most people get. A credit card application, a Holiday Inn promotion, a Book of The Month Club catalog and an invitation to the Blast Off Comic Book Convention in the now completely redesigned wasteland of Los Angeles. At the very bottom of the small pile of junk and brochures was a hand-written envelope. A fan's letter. By virtue of the awkward penmanship and numerous misspellings that appeared on the face of the envelope, I determined the would-be correspondent to be a child, probably not even in the fourth grade. I'd have ordinarily just chucked it on the spot, as I do not take fan mail at my home. (That's what the mail room at id Comics was for, after all.) Then the thought occurred to me that if the child had sent the letter to the New York offices, it would have been destroyed already that morning along with the rest of that city. There was no return address. *Who knows where this kid lived?* I thought. *Maybe he was in one of Captain Steel's cities.* I enthusiastically tore open the envelope, intent on finding out who the child was. I needed some delightfulness that day. Something positive. I wanted to lose myself in it, even if just for a moment. The letter represented what my world had been a mere 24 hours prior and I felt a desperation to return to that time, like Gatsby trying to win back his frothy ex. With the destruction of both New York and L.A., the only major comic book company left standing was Dark Horse Comics out of Milwaukee, Oregon. But there probably wasn't going to be any new comic books printed in a long while (and certainly not ones featuring Captain Steel). The letter inside was written in pencil on a torn-off sheet of notebook paper. It read

deer jony,
bet yoo never thawt yood here of me, did jaw? i see that yoo work for id comics and yoor name is in alot of my captin steel comics bet yoo thinck yoor priDdy smart, doe ncha? i don't no why yoo stoped being my frenD wen we wer kids why did yoo stop being my frend, jon? yoo and me were good frens you liked to com over an wAtch movys with me and play donky kong an jus tawk i liked tawkng with yoo abowd comic books and yoo liked to tawk to me aBowt comic books but in hi scool yoo and me didnt tawk at al
but im not riting to yoo abowt that im riting becaws i hav somthing to tell yoo i am freeing capten steel! i wil free him tomoroh nite wen it is midnite
he is in the eidolon zon rite now, but he tawks to me an he tells me that i can free him by doing what the grimwa says. he 1st started tawking to me a yeer ago in my drems and now he tawks to me wen i am awak. yoo shod here wat he sez, jon. He's reely smart smarter then yoo you think yoo no capten steel but yoo dont no a god damed thing! he nos a lot of god dammed things and he sed that god is a fool.

Wen he coms back from the eidelon zon yoo
will see him an yoo wil thank me for bringin him
back

yoor old frend
timmy

ps i liv in Gale again and if you wanto com over thats
ok but mom mite be meen

I had to read the letter twice to make sure I
was interpreting things correctly. I remembered
Timmy's writing as having improved past this level
by high school. It seemed clear that his ability to
communicate had since degenerated. I examined the
letter and envelope more closely. I was confused. I
thought he had moved to Milwaukee with his mother.
Gale was a 45 minute drive from Madison. I left a
note on the door for the cleaning lady and headed for
Gale in my Jetta.

XI.
I had a full tank of gas. "This is a good thing,"
I told the windshield. *Gas is going to be absolutely
priceless now that the world economy has gone down
the shitter*, my thoughts continued. The drive to Gale
took an hour and forty-five minutes because heavy
traffic along the interstate and connecting highways
forced me to take a back-roads route. The weather,
which had turned rainy and grey, also slowed me
down. That was just fine with me, though. It gave me
some more time to think about Timmy's letter. The
letter had been post-marked three days ago. This was

in keeping with his claim that he was going to "free" Captain Steel the following night, which would have been the night before everything happened. Then there was the contents of the letter itself; Captain Steel had been visiting him in his dreams. That could be attributed to a psychosis of some kind. This psychosis was most likely in the works or in place back when we were kids. I had been right in thinking that he was disturbed back in the school library. *I hate it when I'm fucking right*, I grumbled repeatedly to myself as I approached Gale. His "hearing" Captain Steel while he was awake would then be a further progression of this psychosis. Any freshman Psych major could tell you that. Hell, any high school drop-out could. That didn't come close to explaining everything, however. For one thing, there was a real Captain Steel on the loose. That was not a hallucination or a psychotropic reaction... unless someone had laced the atmosphere with LSD and placed subliminal messages everywhere in an effort to give the world a mass delusion. No one, and surely not Timmy, was capable of that grandiose a plan. Sometimes having a fertile and vivid imagination really sucks. With my mind starting to get wild with looping and overlapping thoughts and impressions, I decided to form a list in my head of what I perceived to be facts;

Fact 1: At 8 a.m. this morning, "Captain Steel" was officially cited.
Fact 2: By noon, he had displayed most of the powers that his comic book counterpart has.

Fact 3: Timmy had sent me a letter which was postmarked three days ago; meaning that it had arrived yesterday, the day before he was to have "freed" Captain Steel.
Fact 4: Despite what I had been told at the reunion, Timmy now lived in his old house in Gale. So did his mother.

The list had done the trick. My mind was clear and organized again, but there was something else Timmy had written that had earned my attention. When I came to the last stop sign before Gale, I pulled out the letter. He had said that Cap was imprisoned in the Eidolon Zone. (The Eidolon Zone, for those of you who don't know, was a device that the comic book Captain Steel sometimes used to temporarily subdue criminals from other worlds. It looked like a big gun that, when used on a villain, opened up a circular vortex portal that sucked the villain into another dimension. While in that dimension, the villain would basically float around in a wraith-like state and never age. It was a good place to tuck villains away after they served their purpose for a given story. But one had to be careful not to put too many villains there, since the Zone was supposed to be pretty much impossible to escape from. Too many prisoners and you run out of bad guys. Too many escapes and the Eidolon Zone loses its mystique.) But that wasn't what had me puzzled. It was something else. A single word. It was a word that stuck out like a sore thumb because the word, if it was supposed to be the word I was thinking of, didn't belong in any discussion concerning Captain Steel.

The word was "grimwa." Phonetically, this Timmy-word resembled "grimoir." A grimoir was not part of the Captain Steel mythos. Captain Steel was based on pseudo-science. He was a man born in the middle of the 24th century and sent back in time as a baby in order to retroactively thwart the plans of a mad scientist, also from his time period. Because the sun put out different radiation levels in his native future, our 20th century atmosphere gave him powers and attributes far exceeding those of ordinary people. A grimoir was a book of magic. It was a tome of spells and, usually satanic, teachings. Nowhere in Captain Steel lore could there be found anything about such a book. Not even those characters who comprised his pantheon of pains-in-the-ass, not even those whose powers were magical (like Dr. Dghpjwx), used a book of magic.

Then there was that line about Captain Steel knowing "a lot of God-dammed things" and God being a "fool." *What was that all about?* I pondered. "Grimoir?" "God is a fool?" What league was he playing in?

I passed right by my old house without stopping, slowing down or looking.

Timmy's tiny house was in bad shape. The lawn was a knee-high jungle of weeds. The blue paint was cracking and flaking off everywhere. The eaves were full of old leaves and the rainwater that they were designed to channel ran out of them like an overflowing tub. The house wasn't much bigger than a trailer home and there was only one, very familiar car in the garage. It belonged to Mrs. Shimmerhorn.

When I knocked on the door, there was no answer. I could already smell the interior of the house. The fragrance was a mixture of Play-Doe, weak air-fresheners and feet. It was a musky, damp smell. I knocked again.

No answer.

I rang the doorbell. (Most people would have done that first, and I didn't realize until just now as I am writing this that ringing the doorbell was something I never did as a kid because Timmy's mom, if you remember, worked nights. Timmy would go ballistic on you if you rang the doorbell, so I never did. It was this habit that guided me to knock first.)

I waited.

I rang the doorbell again.

The inner door opened.

Then the outer screen door opened.

It was Greta Shimmerhorn

and she was huge. When we were kids, she had been a sturdy woman... not fat, just a little overweight. Now she resembled a dumpster and it suddenly occurred to me where all of Timmy's food went. Her head and neck were as grotesquely wide as Timmy's own were narrow. Her hair was in curlers and she was wearing a furry blue robe, stretched tight. Her puffy eyes told me that she had just been indulging in the soothing pleasantries of deep sleep and that I had rather suddenly and rudely yanked her back into the drudgery of the real world. She looked at me with squinting eyes, studying my features. When the shotgun of dawning realization had scored a direct hit and she recognized who I was, her puffy eyes registered this fact, but she continued to squint. That squinting escalated to a narrow-eyed scowl.

"Johnny Boyle," she said, " what... are... YOU... doing... here?" Her voice was a rake clawing gravel.

"Timmy sent me a letter. Asked me to visit him."

"I take care of my Timmy's mail and I haven't sent you anything," she said matter-of-factly.

I held up the empty envelope and she glared at it.

"That's Timmy's handwriting," she reluctantly confirmed. "Let me see the letter."

"No. Where's Timmy?"

"Don't you tell me 'no,' Johnny. Your mother won't like hearing about this when I call her."

I stared at her for a second to make sure she was serious. "Greta, my mother and her feelings concerning my attitude are irrelevant. Where is your son?"

"You run home now. Timmy's watching the Sci-Fi Channel and he doesn't want to be disturbed."

"Then why did he send me a letter saying it was okay to come over for a visit?"

"What letter? He never sent you a letter! I'd know!"

"Greta..."

"And don't you call me 'Greta!' Adults can call me 'Greta.' You kids can call me 'Mrs. Shimmerhorn!'"

"Greta, I'm thirty-one years old and so is Timmy. Now, go and tell him that I'm here and that I need to talk to him about Captain Steel. If he wants, I'll sign some of his comics."

"If I do this, will you give me the letter?"

"If you tell him I'm here and I see him then, yes, you can have the letter."

She frowned. "All right. But you wait right here." She then disappeared into the house.

Their home, as I said, was small. I could hear her tromping and stomping down the stairs that led to that partially finished off basement which had always been the base of operations for Timmy Underachievement Inc.. I could hear her voice her concerns down there, though I couldn't make out what exactly she was saying. Timmy's voice was so feeble that I could hardly hear it at all. In fact, I wasn't even sure I *could* hear it. Then the tromping and stomping resumed. I straightened out and made sure my posture wasn't that of a snoop with a cocked ear. She waddled up to the door.

"Come in," she said with a fake smile.

"Thank you, Mrs. Shimmerhorn."

"Would you like something to drink?"

"No, I'm fine"

"All right. Well, he's down in the basement." She pointed a thick finger to the door off of the kitchen.

"Thanks."

The kitchen contained piles upon piles of full garbage bags heaped up in the corners and under the kitchen table. They made the place a landfill to the nose. As I walked the four steps it took to get to the basement door, I noticed that the kitchen floor was attempting to cling to my shoes. I looked down and saw why; the floor was covered with about a quarter inch of old floor wax. Greta never was much of a housekeeper. As I opened the door into the basement, I noticed that the lights were out down there except for the television, which continually projected light of ever-shifting intensity on the walls and ceiling. The stairs creaked as I traversed them, though not as loudly as when Greta had done so.

Timmy's back was to me as he sat in his old recliner in front of the TV stand. The TV had nothing on it but lightning and static.

His hair was grey and stringy. As I neared him, he did not move. Surrounding him were empty Hostess wrappers and bowls of half-eated oatmeal.

From behind, I could hear Mrs. Shimmerhorn beginning to use the stairs. Slowly.

I whispered Timmy's name.

No response.

I whispered his name again, more loudly this time, as I circled around in front of him. That was when I froze. Timmy's only movements were his shallow chest heaves and his occasional eye blinks. He was *gone* otherwise. Stuck in his nose was a feeding tube, the kind that went down your post-nasal cavity and into your esophagus. It looked like it had been forced in because their was dried blood under his nostrils and along the tube. Next to him was a stand with a bag of fluid. (Timmy's mother was a nurse.) Shrouded to the shoulders in a wool blanket, Timmy was otherwise as I imagined he would be; Dachau revisited. His skin, I could tell even by the poor light of the television set, hadn't been touched by the sun in years. He was looking at the TV, but he wasn't watching it. In retrospect, I think he might have been looking beyond it, if that makes any sense to you. His eyes were half-rolled up... zombie-like. (It was then that I mentally confirmed that it had indeed been him at that the ChicagoCon two years earlier.) He was oblivious to my being present. Oblivious to everything except the light of the TV screen. I took a step back and then, while taking in the whole, miserable, pathetic picture, I realized that there was something wrong under the blanked that covered him. I peeled back the blanket to find even less of Timmy than expected. His half-naked body had four stumps. Four stumps where there should have been scrawny, boney arms and legs. Each one ended in a clean, precise and cauterized cut. A *laser* cut.

And that was when Mrs. Shimmerhorn tackled me.

I landed on the damp floor with the full weight of her girth on top of me. Her fingers were laced into my hair and she used that leverage to slam my head into the thinly carpeted cement. She was breathing heavy but not making more sound than that as she straddled me. My knee instinctively came up and bluntly impacted against her vagina. Nothing happened, so I repeated that maneuver again and again and again. She gasped and rolled over and off of me but didn't let go of my hair. My hands gradually negotiated my hair's release from her grip. Spinning up to my feet as fast as I could, I looked around for something to protect myself with and found nothing. She was slowly making her way up to her feet.

Timmy was indifferent to the situation.

"I don't like you, Johnny Boyle," she huffed. "You don't deserve to be my Timmy's friend. He was never anything but a friend to you and you abandoned him. He was a good boy and you betrayed him for no reason. You were the only friend he had for a long time."

I balled my hands into fists. Those seemed to be my only weapons. "Who were his other friends?"

"The boys in black, but I didn't like them either. They were bad. They would always come and take my Timmy away for a weekend or a week. They made him dye his hair grey." She lunged at me again, screeching "They made his hair grey!!" I didn't have any place to dodge to because of the clutter. She and I tumbled into an old couch nearby and I could hear its frame snap under that sudden stress. I was stuck between the back of the couch and her vast bulk. She was frantically swatting at me with open hands. I blocked them as best I could and then jabbed her in the face. Her nose flattened and sprouted blood. Then she stopped for a second and patted her nose. I used that pause to scramble out from under her. When she saw the blood she pivoted in my direction with a bewildered look. I was standing now and I suddenly remembered that I *did* indeed have a weapon... one that wouldn't kill her but would surely keep her at bay long enough to get the answers I came for. I unfastened by leather belt and pulled it out of the loops. Then I raised it like a whip above my head and brought it down squarely right down the center of her forehead and face with a wet "CRACK!"

That didn't agree with her.

Nor did the next one, which put the metal buckle hard against the left side of her head, at the temple. The next impact she experienced was when her face hit the floor.

I stood there and breathed. She was out, at least for a little while. I went for the phone to dial the police but then remembered that the world had changed. There was no Washington D.C. and, therefore, no federal government. Probably no state or local either. The chaos that the new world was experiencing at that moment, I thought, must have been just as surreal as what I'd seen in that basement. What was she going to do? Call the police on *me?* Nope. Not while she kept a man down there who clearly needed full medical attention. That was assuming the police would even respond to a domestic call during this crisis. So I waited for her to come to. I waited with my belt in hand.

In the next room, off of the TV room, Timmy had created something on the floor. It kind of looked like a pentangle but had a more complex design, like multiple pentangles overlapping with other archaic looking geometric forms surrounding it. There were unlit candles everywhere as well and books. Mostly role playing books and his old children's fantasy storybooks. Lying next to the strange multi-symbol on the floor, however, was something that I knew I simply *had* to take with me.

When Greta Shimmerhorn woke up, she told me what she knew. She had come home from work that morning and found Timmy in front of the TV set in his current autistic state, with no arms and legs. He wouldn't answer her and when she tried to feed him, he was too disassociated to eat. So she drove back to her hospital in Tomah and came back with the food tube paraphernalia. I didn't bother asking her why she didn't call someone, the police or 911. She started to whimper and then begged me to let her see Timmy's letter. She was still laying on the floor and hadn't noticed that her robe had come undone and that she was showing me her titanic, 51-year-old breasts. Some of her greying hair had also fallen out of the curlers and was dangling in front of her sobbing and rapidly bruising face. I reached into my pocket, pulled out the letter and tossed it to her.

"I'm leaving now," I said.

XII.

I don't know exactly when I lost consciousness. Somewhere in the neighborhood of the half-way point between my former home and my adopted home is what I'm guessing at this point. I don't know quite for how long, either, but it was long enough.

I was driving back to Mad-town, trying to compose lists in my head again. The disorder there (in my head) was mounting. My rather emotionless treatment of Greta Shimmerhorn was not exactly the robotic act it had seemed. But that wasn't it. *Timmy... Jesus*, I started to think. I tried not to. I tried to think about something else, but there wasn't something else.

Timmy, oh Christ, there's nothing left, that mom of yours, nothing but TV, that's all you were; comic books and TV and junk food and bad fiction, all you were, and now you're less, less, Les Lincoln,

*Lincoln memorial gone, Greta did this, I let it happen,
no legs now, no arms, bloody feeding tube, just let
him die...*

I'm guessing that the deaths of millions of
people at the hands of a character with whom I was
intimately familiar also had something to do with the
lessening of gravity's effect on my head.

It was snowing.

Or so it seemed.

Not the kind you get on Christmas morning.

No.

The kind you get when you try to watch a pay
channel that you haven't subscribed to.

Then it sounded like I was wearing ear plugs.

I swerved to the side of the old farm road and
then

I was at home. Back in Gale, some time ago.
It was my old bedroom, at night. I was lying on my
bed with that week's issues sprawled out this is
strange because I could clearly see the reading chair
that my folks had gotten for me to prevent me from
reading on my stomach once that chair was in my
room I never laid on my bed to read again but here I
was now doing it just the same with the chair in plain
sight the comic I was looking at didn't look familiar
and didn't read very well all dream writing does not
read very well the pictures didn't make sense either as
though each panel had been gleaned from another
comic book entirely then I got the premonition that I
was not alone my premonition was given credence by
a tearing sound coming from the floor at the foot of
my bed.

I maneuvered myself to that end and peered over the edge.

The green hand had already forced it's way up from whatever netherworld was just beneath my blue bedroom carpet, when my eyes had peeked over the edge of my bed, the second green hand was emerging as well then, once both hands had a firm measure of leverage in this world, they pulled the rest of Lou Ferrigno up through my bedroom floor Lou Ferrigno with green skin he was in his season one make-up... the most inhuman design that Universal had come up with during the show's run once he had fully entered my room, he stood there and stared. No growling no flexing no angry faces, he just stood his full 6'3" height and stared at me with those white eyes, he was angry, I could tell, but he was a quiet angry a patient angry.

Then the ceiling collapsed in a nice, tight, downward explosion, the ceiling had given way thanks to feet clad in shiny, well-polished shoes, as the feet descended to the carpeted floor and made contact, the dust rapidly cleared to reveal a sharply dressed man with a kind face, he was wearing a conservative business suit, an eye-patch and a fedora, Lou was indifferent to Kirk Alyn's arrival, as though he had been expecting it, Kirk Alyn (as Les Lincoln, the secret identity of Captain Steel) was, of course, in black and white just as he had appeared on the screen in the days of old, he too was angry in a way that the character never was. His eyes were angry.

Then my bedroom door was kicked apart by a red and white boot and Linda Carter took her place next to the other two, walking over the rapidly fading shards of wood from the fallen door, she was, despite her brilliant star-spangled outfit, not looking too *wonder*ful.

The final one to enter my room was John Wesley Shipp, who vibrated through the far wall in a blood-red blur (a trademark technique of character he used to play on television).

I was surrounded. Naked now. Horrified.

It was them, but it was *not* them.

Then Les Lincoln, now being played by Reed Christopherson in full Technicolor, spoke.

He told me that I only *thought* I knew them.

He told me that they were going do what they wanted.

He told me that they wanted to kill everyone because they hated everyone.

He told me that it was right.

Bill Bixby (formerly Lou) snarled.

Linda Carter let out an orgasmic shriek.

John Wesley Shipp laughed in slow motion.

I cowered.

And my comic books bled.

I woke in a cold sweat that made my face slide off of the steering wheel. The clock said I'd been gone for only five minutes but had felt much longer. I could still hear the lingering remains of slow motion laughter coming from the book that I had confiscated from Timmy's basement.

XIII

Timmy might've died of shock if the TV had been knocked over during our little struggle, I reflected as I finished driving home along the same twisting, winding roads that had brought me one last time to Gale, Wisconsin. *How many cities across the globe has Captain Steel destroyed by now?* I wondered. *He probably started with London or Madrid and worked his way east.* "He'll have a field day in Russia," I told my dashboard. *And wait until he hits Japan! Maybe Godzilla'll show up too.* I abruptly started giggling, but then remembered the dream. There was nothing on the radio except for one local AM news station and they were reading reports directly off of the Associated Press wire and other sources. (You can't get much radio reception while driving through the coulees of Wisconsin.) Captain Steel had spared Atlanta, the headquarters of CNN, so news was still coming in from them, but their news had to go through indirect and slightly slower information pipelines now. There was no doubt in my mind that Steel would return to the U.S. and would eventually finish what he had started here. The sun was just starting to set when I got back to Madison.

As I approached my house, I could see that it was surrounded by an unusual number of unusual vehicles. Some were military and others were ordinary but had government plates. When I opened my car door and got out, I was greeted by a very serious man in a business suit flanked by two grunts in cammies.

"Mister Boyle?" said the g-man.

"Hugh bet'cha!" I jovially replied. I really didn't give a fuck about a whole Hell of a lot at that point.

"Sir, you're coming with us."

"Sure. But, ah... *why?*"

"Not here, sir. The sky has ears... as I'm sure you're aware."

XIV.

I spent about an hour in an armored van, which also transported four other g-men dressed very much the same way as the first. Then I was transferred to a helicopter and in that I was shipped to an air strip with a big, weird-looking jet parked on it. I boarded the jet and it was then that the lead g-man decided it was okay to let me in on the nature of our trip. He was a plain looking man of average height and build with no overtly distinguishing features. He was the kind of man who blended in.

"We need you," said the g-man. "We need you to help us formulate a defensive strategy against Captain Iron."

"Captain *Steel*," I corrected.

"Captain Steel."

"A *defensive* strategy? I thought you guys would be more interested in coming up with an *offensive* strategy."

The g-man's mouth flexed into a smirk and he replied, "Well Mr. Boyle, as a writer you should be familiar with the concept of the 'cliche.' Our favorite cliche is 'there's no defense like a good offense.'"

"Ah," I nodded.

XV.

I don't know where they took me. I asked my escorts and they politely told me not to ask again. So I didn't. It was someplace underground, I gathered, because I never did see a window once I got there. When they had given me a quiet moment in some sort of lounge/waiting area, the g-man who had accompanied me during the whole trip (the one who could blend in) asked me if I thought there was anyone else who might be able to aid in the effort. I told him that I'd like Simon Smythe's opinion about the thing I had confiscated from the Shimmerhorn house, which I produced from my duffle bag and laid on the table. He looked at the old book as it lay on the table, then he turned his attention back to me in robotic fashion. "Smythe's another associate professor at Madison," I explained, "He teaches History Gen-Eds but his hobbies are demonology and that kinda stuff. I think he might be helpful if you can get him."

"We'll have him here in ninety minutes," the g-man said as he brought his cell phone to his ear.

XVI.

Now, I could go on and on about what this place was like as well as all the stuff they gave me to read about the situation (which most people now already know, I'm sure). But I won't go into those things here. That's for the book... if, as I said earlier, it turns out that I'm not presently dying of super-cancer.

Anyway, a very shaken-up Simon Smythe ended up seated next to me around a big table also accommodating politicians, scientists, generals, admirals and more g-men. (It was the War Room from "Dr. Strangelove.") For the purposes of security,

I doubt that the government would let me list the names of any of them, so I won't bother.

Then the Vice President walked in. He was the acting President by then, after D.C., but he didn't seem to mind that we all addressed him as "Vice President." Maybe it wasn't official yet. Or maybe he was rightfully more interested in the subject at hand. The VP took his seat and began by saying

"Gentlemen, we've got to act fast. Captain Steel is currently making short work of Russia and it won't take him long to plow through the rest of Asia and then back here, if he continues on his present course and speed. You've all been briefed on the status of our nation's resources and the readiness of our armed forces." He paused and glanced at us all. "It's time for a plan of action, gentlemen. What have you got?"

Oh, please keep in mind that this is not verbatim. This meeting is written as best as I can remember it.

A four-star admiral, who must have been the acting senior military advisor, started talking immediately and aggressively. "The Air Force failed to eliminate the hostile at Los Angeles using conventional weapons such as incendiaries, anti-aircraft ammunition and stingers. I recommend deploying our nuclear ordnance. We can launch a full scale attack while he is making his way across the Pacific. Ecological damage would be a concern, but it's better to attack him there as opposed to on American soil. Now, we can deliver-"

"That won't do a damn thing," I blurted out, interrupting the Admiral.

All eyes were now on me.

"And why the damn Hell not, Mister...?" the Admiral asked, squinting to see my name tag from across the table.

"Captain Steel can withstand any nuclear weapon you've got," I declared. "Last year I wrote a story in which a 40 megaton nuke went off in his arms and all it did was render him unconscious for a few minutes."

The Vice President was listening.

The Admiral was not. "*Mister* Boyle. I wasn't responsible for you being here and I am of the opinion that bringing you to this meeting was a profound waste of valuable fuel. I know what our weapons are capable of a helluva lot better than you and further; what we are dealing with is not 'Captain Steel' because there is, I'm sorry to break this to you, no... such... person... as 'Captain Steel.'"

"All right, Admiral," I calmly countered. "Then who or what is it?"

The Admiral didn't have an answer for that and tried to continue with his description of the nuclear weapon idea (read: joke). The Vice President cut him off, however, and asked him to move on to another plan.

"Another plan, Sir, is our 'Star Wars' orbiting peace platform. It's designed, as most of us know," he glared at me for a second there, "to destroy intercontinental ballistic missiles with a focused, high-powered laser beam."

"That won't work either," I interrupted. "One of the Captain's frequent enemies in the comic books is Madam Microwave and her laser weapons can saw continents in half. He's withstood her entire arsenal."

"'Madam.. *Microwave*?'" repeated the Admiral.

"Furthermore," I continued, "the simple fact that he can produce lasers of equal power from his *eyes* suggests that his body is more than capable of withstanding yours."

"That's enough of you wasting our time with this nonsense, Boyle-" snapped the Admiral.

I didn't stop. "Gentlemen, 'nonsense' is *precisely* what we are dealing with. Doctor Smythe and I have worked out the generals as to how this entity came about and I think that *that* is crucial in helping us find an exploitable vulnerability."

"I agree," said the Vice President. "What have you got?" I suddenly got the impression that the VP might have been a comic book fan once.

"Just prior to my... *recruitment* into this particular little group, I had done a little investigating on my own. As fate would have it, the origin of this particular Captain Steel is the direct fault of a childhood friend of mine named Timmy Shimmerhorn. Timmy was an obsessed comic book fan ever since he was a small child and this grew to become part of his developing psychosis. Shimmerhorn's schizophrenia was based on the notion that superheroes existed and were all his friends. He didn't have many real friends, you see, so he created ones in his mind. This general trend is fairly common in the realm of psychological illnesses, and for one or more reasons, Timmy was never diagnosed with a problem. Timmy's maturity and health were also subnormal. What I've been able to piece together with the help of this facility's data base is that, sometime after his eighteenth birthday, Shimmerhorn and his mother moved to Milwaukee when she accepted a job there as a head nurse. Timmy's weak and malleable state-of-mind allowed a local occult group there to initiate him fully into their ranks and brainwash him to a degree. Sometime later, this same group all apparently committed mass suicide, with the exception of Timmy. The police investigation that followed revealed that the group may have been involved heavily in demon worship and probably human sacrifice. Timmy's mother had a nervous breakdown soon after that and ended up giving a patient the wrong dosage of intravenous drugs. She was dismissed and the only place where she could find work in nursing was back at the small hospital where she had worked for previously, in Tomah, Wisconsin. The hospital was ran by a friend of hers and strings were pulled and documents forged to allow her to continue doing the work she had trained for."

Everybody was paying complete attention... even the Admiral and his good ol' boys. "Hawks," to all of you baby boomers out there.

"I received a letter from Timmy yesterday morning and it specified that he had been in contact with Captain Steel and that he was going to attempt to free him from the Eidolon Zone."

About half of those in attendance nodded slightly, indicating that they knew what the Eidolon Zone was. The others got a brief explanation.

"I went to Timmy's house and found him in a vegetative state and with no arms and legs. His limbs had been sliced off cleanly and cauterized at the same time. This is in keeping with the properties of Captain Steel's laservision. Having searched his dwelling, I found the book that Timmy used to summon 'Captain Steel.' It's called the Soggoth Grimoir and I figure he must have pinched it from his fellow cult members while he was in Milwaukee. It's a book of black magic that has eluded the various authorities of man throughout history."

"He used a book of black magic to create a superhero?" asked the Vice President with a raised eyebrow.

Now it was Simon's turn. "This entity is not a superhero, obviously. It's a *demon*. I've gone over the book and I'm convinced that the incantation Shimmerman used is the one for the conjuring of a ghackodaemon."

Nobody recognized the term.

"A ghackodaemon is a special variety of demon. It is an ectoplasmic lifeform that can come into this world, but first it has to be summoned and assigned a form to take. The person performing the incantation selects the physical form of the demon. The demon then steps out of the netherworld and into our world as whomever the practitioner wishes it to resemble. The ghackodaemon retains the look, skills, physical abilities and even some of the habits of the chosen form"

I needed to briefly interrupt Simon at that point. "You see, Timmy believed in his mind that Captain Steel was a real person. When he started reading that section of the book, the demon was given license to communicate with him, first through his dreams and then, as Timmy became more and more seduced by the book, it was able to communicate with Timmy while he was conscious. It lied to him and convinced him that it was Captain Steel, trapped in the Captain's own extradimensional prison... which had a ring of truth in it because that is exactly what the netherworld is to an entity like this. A prison."

Back to Simon. "Y'see this incantation was originally designed to take advantage of someone who had lost a loved one. A lover or a grieving parent or child would be lulled into performing the ceremony by the prospect of seeing their deceased loved one again. The ghackodaemon then comes to Earth like I said and proceeds to do evil works, like any other evil creature would. Let's say, for example, that Houdini's widow had used this incantation in an effort to see her late husband again. What would have come through the gate would have been a semblance of Harry Houdini that would have possessed all of his skills at escape and showmanship. But this spell was never designed to give a ghackodaemon the form of a fictional character."

"Hard to believe a guy with 'subnormal' maturity coulda been smart enough to read a book like that," the Admiral grumbled.

"The Soggoth Grimoir's text appears to shift into whatever language the reader is most comfortable with," said Simon. "I understand both Latin and Celtic languages and when I examined the book, the words shifted between those and English. I put it to the test and had one of your interpreters read a passage from it an hour ago. She said it was in Japanese."

"That's a fascinating story, gentlemen, and I have no doubt that *that's* what happened," said the Vice President. "Satellite first spotted the Captain flying over central Wisconsin, so that corroborates with your hypothesis and turns it into a good working theory. It's the theory that we're going to go with." Simon and I looked at each other when he said that. We didn't know about that satellite data. The VP continued. "So, now that we know what we're dealing with, how do we put it down?"

Simon took a deep breath and said, "I don't know, Mr. Vice President. The ghackodaemon would normally be killed just like any mortal man would be killed. Its body is made of ectoplasm molded into the selected form and acts accordingly when subjected to lethal force. But, again, Shimmerhorn didn't give it the form of a real person. He gave it the form of a fictional character."

The room was silent for a long moment. Those in attendance were deep in thought, looking for inspiration in the table and the papers that coated it. They found none.

The Vice President closed his eyes and said, "Then it's hopeless." He paused and then continued. "I remember reading the *Captain Steel* comic books when I was a boy and I can remember reading stories where he pushed planets out of orbit, drank the ocean in a single gulp and lifted entire mountain ranges. He could travel through *time* for God's sake! How are we going to fight something that can do all of those things?"

"Smythe, what if you performed the same spell and created another ghackowhatever?" asked the Admiral. "We might be able to get them to fight and destroy each other. Maybe an arch enemy of Captain Steel's?"

Simon looked at the Admiral flatly. "Admiral, Captain Steel is the greatest superhero in cartoon Americana and look what this entity has done. Now, that being the case, what makes you think that conjuring another creature like it would be anything even *remotely* akin to a good idea?"

"Besides," I added. "Only someone as mentally ill as Timmy could have created Captain Steel using this book. We'd need someone who is just as delusional."

The Admiral abruptly altered the subject. "I still don't see why one of our laser platforms can't kill him. These lasers can cut through solid steel!"

"So?" I asked.

"Whadda ya mean 'so?' He's called 'Captain *Steel*,' right? As in 'strong as steel?'"

I had to explain to the Admiral that when the character was first created in the 30's, he was as durable as steel. Nothing short of an exploding grenade could open his skin. Over the years, however, the character's durability gradually evolved so as to make him far more durable than steel. The character's name stuck even though it no longer really applied like it originally had.

The Admiral didn't give up. "All right, he's called '*Captain* Steel,' right? Well what if someone of higher rank gave him an order? Like me. He'd have to obey it, right?"

Everybody sighed. This just wasn't the Admiral's moment to shine. That would come later.

"Mr. Vice President, I don't think he's as powerful as the version you remember," I said.

The VP's eyes flew open with a glimmer of hope.

"Would I be right in assuming that the comics you read as a boy were published prior to 1986?" I asked.

"Yes," he replied.

"That's a good thing. You see, Timmy's collection of comics was mostly Post-Catastrophe. Do you follow?"

The VP shook his head.

"In 1986, id Comics saw that their sales were dropping and, in an effort to make their characters more exciting, Captain Steel in particular, they revamped their characters and did what we in the comic book industry call a 'retcon.' 'Retcon' is short for 'retroactive continuity.' The story that kicked off the whole event was called 'Catastrophe on Multiple Earths.' They took the Captain Steel character and modified him slightly in order to appeal to modern readers. They lessened his powers so that he wasn't so unbeatable and, in doing so, made his stories more entertaining. The modern version can't do a lot of the things that you remember from your old comics... things like drinking the ocean and time traveling. Timmy's collection was mostly from the Post-Catastrophe era because Pre-Catastrophe comics are rare and too valuable for someone without a job to buy. Therefore, this Captain's powers would most likely reflect the newer, lesser powered version."

"So he's not invulnerable?" asked the VP.

"Well, yes, for all practical purposes he *is* still invulnerable," I replied. "But he isn't virtually *omnipotent* like he was before 1986."

"Okay," one of the g-men said in a frustrated tone, "what powers *does* he have?"

I listed them. The comic book Captain Steel could fly, move faster than the eye could follow, lift something as heavy as a battleship (I used that comparison for the benefit of the Admiral), fire lasers from his eyes, exhale tremendous freezing winds, hear and see at superhuman levels and he could see through things at will. Then I listed the other "unofficial" powers he had; Captain Steel could lift an object (like said battleship) without destroying it in the process. He could fly at supersonic speeds without shredding his costume. He can talk in outer space (despite the lack of an atmosphere).

The three-star General sitting next to the Admiral spoke up, saying "You said nukes and lasers won't work on him. What will?"

"The comic book Captain Steel has three specific vulnerabilities and one limitation.". Some in attendance probably already knew what these were. Captain Steel's weaknesses are about as well known as those of movie vampires. "His limitation is that he can't see through anything made of zinc or that is zinc-plated. As for his actual weaknesses, the comic book Captain is vulnerable, like all things are, to magic... but since *this* particular Captain Steel is pretty much *made of* magic, I don't think that's an option. The second weakness is to a radioactive substance called 'neonite,' but since there's no such thing as neonite, that's not an option either. And the third one, we can pretty much forget about too."

"Why? What is it?" asked the VP.

"His third weakness is that he is powerless under the rays of a green sun, like the one in his native future," I said. "I'm just guessing here, but I'd say that there's no practical way we can make the sun green."

"And I think you would be right about that," confirmed the VP.

"Now wait a minute," interjected the Admiral. "The *color* of the sun can take away his powers?"

"More or less, yeah," I answered. "The sun's color is indicative of its energy output a-"

"Yeah yeah yeah, I understand the idea behind it," said the Admiral. "But this demon-thing isn't *really* getting his powers from the sun. He's basically just pretending to be a guy who does, right?"

I was beginning to see the Admiral's point. He continued. "So if the sun turned green, even if it really wasn't caused by a change in radiation levels, he would still get weaker, right?"

Simon answered his question, saying, "Right. This entity would suffer from what's called a 'psychosomatic reaction.' This is basically how all demons are killed or hurt. It's like a reverse placebo. Their bodies are only partially corporeal, yet fully corporeal things like silver can kill them depending on what kind of demon we're talking about. Psychosomatic reactions are also how some daemons develop lesions when they're touched by mistletoe. They develop them because that is what's *supposed* to happen and their ectoplasmic bodies react accordingly, even if, scientifically, there is no real reason for the reaction. A ghackodaemon would die from a stab wound, not because the knife actually harmed his supernatural body, but because the knife would have killed the being he is modeled after. Likewise, this Captain Steel'd loose his powers, not because of anything having to do with the sun's radiation, but because he's simply *supposed* to lose his powers under the rays of a green sun according to the parameters of his current form. I think."

The VP looked at Simon. "You *think*?"

"We're talking about magic here, sir. Magic is not based on logic or scientific principles. We're never going to know for sure how this thing will react to something like that until we actually see it happen."

A Navy lieutenant then burst in with an urgent look on his face. He told us that the Russians had sent a few photos via the internet. The Lieutenant instructed us to look at a large TV screen nearby. On the screen appeared a series of rather puzzling images. They looked like they were taken from a helicopter and showed the Captain hovering next to a large Russian office building. In all of the pics, the Captain appeared as a red, blue and yellow blur in the general form of a man.

"Why is it that none of the photographs taken of him can capture any details?" asked one frustrated general.

I offered my hypothesis. "He's vibrating. Unlike most superheroes, Captain Steel doesn't wear a mask when he's in costume. As Les Lincoln, he wears an eye-patch as a disguise. Back in the thirties, this was fine, but to a modern audience that idea is rather weak. So, the editorial staff told the writers of the Captain Steel titles to come up with a way to further explain why nobody recognizes Les Lincoln as Captain Steel. One of the things the writers came up with to explain this was to establish that Captain Steel never allows himself to be photographed. He vibrates his body so that the images people take of him are blurry."

The last photograph in the series was the strangest. All of the pics were virtually the same and seemed to have been taken by a high speed camera. They all showed the Captain hovering in the same position next to the Russian office building. But the last one had us all scratching our heads. Even me. It was the same as the others, except in the background there was an optical anomaly. It was shaped like two circles partially overlapping. What was depicted inside this shape appeared to be a magnification of the inside of the building.

The VP turned to me. "What's that?"

I stared at it, still confused. "He's... looking through the walls. (?)"

A g-man a few seats down from me said, "That doesn't make sense. The *camera* isn't looking through the building. *He* is."

"But we can see it," said Simon. "Just like a comic book reader can see what Captain Steel is looking at when he uses this power... so can we. I had no idea that the spell would interpret the character's powers so *literally.* "

"Literal" was right. It was too literal. Instead of looking through things, the Captain was, in effect, making whatever he looked at transparent. But this interpretation wasn't in violation of the comic book. It was actually hyper-accurate.

There was something else that I noticed in one of the other photographs, but I didn't share it with the rest of the team. It was off in the upper left-hand corner and it looked like another anomaly, though one that had all but faded away by the time the camera's shudder had opened and shut.

These photos brought about new enthusiasm for the green sun idea.

The Admiral turned to the VP. "Sir, NASA might be able to rig some kind of filter of gas or what-not that could make the sun appear green on Earth."

"If we had more time, Admiral, I'd agree with you. But Captain Steel will be here the day after tomorrow and I don't think we can get a shuttle into orbit in that time." The VP continued in his mood of hopelessness, saying "The irony of this situation is just... *staggering*. Our country and the rest of the world is being destroyed by one of our favorite symbols for truth, freedom and the American Dream.." He continued to mope like this for several minutes while scientists and personnel continually gave us updates.

A civilian scientist in attendance suddenly looked up and asked me to describe neonite to him. "Neonite's a purple ore or element that's deadly to the Captain," I told him. "Its specific radiation patterns reduce his powers down to minimal levels and, after being exposed to it for a flexible duration of time, he is supposed to die from it." He asked what I meant by "flexible." I replied, "Well, the Captain's never actually died from neonite exposure because he's got to sell comic books the following month. In the stories, he always escapes the neonite or the neonite gets taken away from him before it can do him in."

The scientist then said, "Gentlemen, my laboratory has just last week created a new element for the periodic table using an atom smasher. It has been assigned a number but not a name as of yet. What if we named it 'neonite?'"

The VP looked at Simon and I. "Gentlemen, would that work?"

"I don't know," we both said in unison.

"Would the Captain have a psychosomatic reaction to this substance if 'neonite' were its official and original name?" asked the VP.

Simon's eyebrows gradually scaled his forehead and he said, "I-I think it might. Yes. Yes! Once the new element is officially designated 'neonite' and he is exposed to it, his body should feel the same affects that the comic neonite has on the comic Captain Steel."

The VP then turned to the scientist. "How soon can you have some for us?"

The scientist adjusted his glasses and said, "My laboratory has a few fragments in storage, but they have to be kept super-cold. Otherwise, they'll decay within a matter of minutes."

I felt my heart suddenly sink. "How many minutes?"

"A fragment the size of a golf ball will completely disintegrate in just under eight minutes at room temperature," he answered. "How long does it *have* to last?"

"Long enough to kill him," I replied.

The Admiral then suggested that a team be assembled. Each team member would be armed with a cold canister containing a fragment of neonite to expose Captain Steel with. That way, if one fragment disintegrated before he was dead, another could be applied. I agreed with that strategy.

Then the Admiral said that Simon and myself would be on said team.

I asked him why.

The Admiral told me that we'd be tagging along because Simon and I knew more about what might be going on inside our foe's head than anyone else. We were the closest things to psychological profilers that there were and we might be needed in order to predict what he might do. I knew more about his physical abilities and Simon could predict better than anyone what he might be thinking and how he would react certain situations. I couldn't really argue with that.

Those assembled were dismissed to get started on the plan. The Admiral stopped me before I got to the door. "How weak will neonite make him?" he inquired in a soft voice.

I told him that in the comic books, neonite begins incapacitating the Captain instantly. His superhuman speed, strength and ability to fly go away and he becomes so dizzy that he can't stand. Other powers, like laservision and x-ray sight, are reduced to minimal levels.

The Admiral's next question of me was, "When he's sick from neonite, can he still stop bullets?"

"No," I answered.

"Good," grinned the Admiral. "I'm sending a SEAL team with you."

There was one last thing that the civilian scientist mentioned before we had completely dispersed from the War Room. He said, "I forgot to mention something. My neonite is highly radioactive and lethal to just about everything, human beings included. That isn't going to be a problem is it?"

XVII.

The plan was simple. Simon, three scientists, a SEAL team of five and myself were to be sent to a remote locale (where radiation from the neonite fragments would harm as few humans and ecological features as possible) and try to attract the Captain to us for the ambush. We figured that if the daemon knew anything about the character it was modeled after, it would believe itself safe and wouldn't expect us to come up with neonite. If the daemon didn't know anything about the character, which was my assumption, then that was even better. He'd become disoriented and begin dying and he wouldn't know the reason why. The villain in me liked the idea of that. (Surprised? Don't be. You can't write melodramatic comic book tales, or most forms of fiction for that matter, without delving into the realm of villainy. A superhero needs a supervillain and the more nasty and evil the supervillain, the more heroic and grand the superhero for stopping said supervillain.) I also enjoyed taking Greta Shimmerhorn down with my leather belt too, by the way. I still don't feel guilty about that because Greta was a monster. Now, I was gearing up to meet another monster. He was a monster for having killed a billion people or more. He was a monster for his freakish abilities. He was a monster for having twisted a heroic image into one that will now be despised forever. Despite the fact that the first of those monstrous qualities was clearly the most significant, I was drawn to the latter one the most. Maybe it was in an unconscious effort not to "psyche myself out" (like what happened when I left Gale). I preoccupied myself with what this entity had done to my favorite job. Superheroes would probably not return when civilization rose from its ashes. I wasn't worried about my own career. I would write more novels. I would survive. The Captain wouldn't, not even in the form of whimsical, fluffy entertainment. Superheroes, as a specific fiction sub-genre, had been destroyed because one of them had become real. No, that's not it. Here's a better one; Superheroes had been destroyed by a pathetic little man-child named Timmy, who loved them more than anything. No one can love something with the same passion as a psycho, after all. 'Course, I should probably say something about his beast mother, too but...

Cripes, I wanted to keep this version short.

Getting back to the plan; it was determined that the Arctic would make the best location for a couple of reasons. First, it was remote. Second, the comic book Captain Steel had a home in the Arctic, the Stronghold of Serenity. Simon believed that the daemon might be attracted to this area because of the original character's familiarity with it. Third, the location provided the perfect opportunity for the Admiral to nuke Captain Steel if the neonite plan didn't work. We had been told that if we failed to kill him for whatever reason, there would be a submarine nearby armed with a SUBROC torpedo. It is my understanding that the SUBROC nuclear-tipped torpedo had been discontinued in the mid-seventies because it was not a practical weapon. Apparently, the Navy hadn't gotten rid of them all.

Just in case Captain Steel didn't have an attraction for the Arctic, another idea was realized. And it was all mine. In the comics, Captain Steel's sweetheart (and later wife) Tenille Trust wore a special locket and inside the locket was an ultrasonic beacon that she could activate whenever she was in trouble. Hearing the beacon, Steel would invariably come to her rescue. My suggestion was that such a similar device be created. At first, the engineers who were working on our equipment didn't get it. They thought that duplicating the frequency was the goal. I said, "No. All you have to do is put an ultrasonic device inside a locket. He answers the call of a locket. The signal frequency and power are inconsequential." So they put a device in a heart-shaped locket that would, when squeezed, put out a dog-whistle sound.

Each member of the team was given a special canister for their neonite. These canisters clipped to our belts and each had a sliding mechanism that would expose the fragments to the atmosphere, and our intended victim. The canisters kept the fragments, which ranged in size from baseballs to softballs, at a constant temperature of zero degrees Kelvin. The canisters were also shields against the intense radioactivity that the neonite produced. That radioactivity was enough to kill a man in under ten minutes. I found it rather eerie that our neonite would kill us about as fast as it was supposed to kill Captain Steel. One final touch was that our neonite was given a light purple hue to match the stuff in the comics. (Don't ask me how they managed to do that. "It's technical," was what they told me when I asked.)

Then there were the suits, which were to provide us protection while we exposed the daemon to the neonite. The suits were cumbersome silver ensembles. They were also designed to keep us warm.

The SEAL team's orders were pretty straightforward: Help the neonite do its job. When he starts to double over and die, help him along.

The SEALS were armed to the teeth.

We were all set.

Shit. I feel like I'm burning up here. I had to stop typing in order to get looked at by the *Sand Lance's* Hospital Corpsman. (I'm really surprised that these subs don't have actual doctors on board.) My blood feels hot. Probably just the flu.

XVIII.

Our transportation to the site of our little ambush was another strange looking jet that went really really fast. We went from wherever the War Room was to the pole in about three hours. Captain Steel was just finishing up Tokyo. Intelligence gave us a briefing and mentioned that the Captain had an affinity for destroying monuments and landmarks. When they asked us why that was, Simon and I both told them "Hell if I know."

When we got to the site, the scientists who were with us set up the observation station and all of the special equipment designed to analyze the daemon. We were lucky. The Arctic was experiencing a near constant state of dusk and we had just enough light in which to work. We all looked like astronauts on some cold asteroid as Simon and I erected the shelters and the SEALs cleaned and set up their gear. Fascinating equipment, by the way. Of particular interest to me were the C4 explosives. I had always thought the stuff was highly volatile and blew up if you set it on fire, like in "Demolition Man" and other action movies, but no. One SEAL, the youngest (couldn't have been more than 18), demonstrated how safe the stuff was by rolling some into a little ball and holding it over his lit Zippo. When I got the "go ahead" from the SEAL lieutenant, I activated the locket.

The Master Chief SEAL was just finishing up explaining to me the difference between standard rifle ammunition and their NATO-compliant, explosive tip, light-armor piercing caseless rounds when Simon came up to me and said he wanted to talk. We walked south about ten paces (any direction you went was south) and then he put his hand on my elbow and showed me how scared he was. His encapsulated face bore the expression of a man who had lost all confidence in the Almighty. "I've been thinking about that Soviet photograph," he said. "The one that showed him using his x-ray sight."

"Soviet Union's been gone for a while now, man," I said. Use of the word "soviet" to describe anything after the establishment of the Commonwealth of Independent States was one of my petty little pet peeves. "What bothered you about it? Something you didn't say while we were on the 'Strangelove' set?"

"Well, it just never really sank in with me until we came here and I felt the cold reality of this place. I'd been handling this like it was happening to someone else."

"I think that's a good way to handle it. That's how I've been handling it. I'm just watching a movie, that's all. Now, what bothered you about the pictures from Minsk?"

"The way in which that vision power of his was interpreted by the Grimoir's spell. This thing's powers aren't the way they should be, y'know? It just makes me wonder about what else we don't know."

"I was thinking that on our way over here too. His x-ray sight manifested itself looking like it does to the *reader* and not the other *characters* in the comics. It raises some fascinating questions."

"I've been thinking. What if we've been wrong and this thing doesn't have anything to do with daemons or Captain Steel? He hasn't been positively identified on film. The only reason we think that is because of eyewitness accounts. Most of those people are dead."

"The Grimoir *did* change languages while you were reading it, right? This we even managed to verify with several others. And Timmy's note was no coincidence. Nor were his wounds. And the things that this Captain Steel can do and the specific building he destroyed first; these were no coincidences either."

"Yeah," Simon sighed as he looked back towards the tents. "Think you'll still be in the comic book business when this is all through? Think you'll still be writing *The Adventures of Captain Steel*?"

"Not a chance, Simon. In any event, I don't think that the medium will recov-"

That was when Simon popped like an overcooked hot dog wiener.

The whole area was green and the rest of our little group shrieked and exploded. I was fine. Then the green went away.

I quickly looked around to see where the green had come from and couldn't see anything for miles around except what remained of our camp. Then realization dawned and I slowly, shakily brought my eyes skyward.

It was descending toward me with the grace of an angel. It slowed to a complete stop about two feet above the snow and hovered. With its arms akimbo, it was less than thirty feet away and did not move. In my chest, I was five years old again and I was desperate for a couch to hide behind.

The thing didn't look like Reed Christopherson. It didn't look like Kirk Alyn. It looked like Captain Steel... and it was *hideous*. A horror to behold, the body was impossibly disproportionate. The shoulders were far too broad and made it look, at first, as though it were wearing football shoulder pads. It wasn't, of course. The neck was too thick to belong to even a steroid abuser. Its jaw and chin made those of the late Jay Leno look weak. The hands were too large. They were also stained brown with dried blood. As my eyes moved down, it became readily apparent to me why this monstrosity always flew and hovered, but never walked or stood. He couldn't. The waist was grotesquely narrow and couldn't possibly support the vast upper body, were this creature not superstrong. The thighs were thicker than the waste and would restrict its movement. The ankles and feet were too thin. His legs were not designed to be used, so he didn't use them.

(In retrospect, I now recognize the artwork that the daemon had been molded to. The artist's name was Rod Truthfield. He was notorious for his extreme exaggeration of bodily proportions.)

I mustered up enough courage to return my gaze to its face. That mannequin face. What I saw there was an unmoving, unbreathing smile. It was the overly broad smile of a comic book superhero proudly posing for a pin-up with his or her cape fluttering in the breeze. But the eyes weren't smiling. They were cursing. It was like looking at a three dimensional painting. Frozen, intense and definitely inhuman. It was at this time that I noticed that its hair was dark blue. This was, of course, because blue was the color that they used in the comics to shade the Captain's black hair. The rest of the characters in the comic books saw it as being black. The Grimoir had not. The texture of the skin was non-existent. The skin was smooth, like porcelain, and seemed bereft of life.

I stared at the evil eyes for what must have been at least a minute or two. The emotions that shifted back and forth in those eyes were those of superiority, hatred, frustration, misery and then back to superiority. I never did see the eyes blink, even with the winter winds whipping between us.

Then words blurted out of my mouth. "Now what?" I asked. My tone matched my attitude. My attitude was that I was about to become a wet pile of human debris littering the Arctic, like the freezing corpses of the rest of the group around us. I was glad to have my mask. The smell was probably that of Hell.

Captain Steel didn't say anything. Didn't move. Didn't breathe. The eyes just continued to study me, as though looking inside me. I looked down and made sure he hadn't turned me transparent with his fucked x-ray sight.

"Nothing to say?" I inquired.

No response.

A few seconds went by.

"Well?!!"

Then Captain Steel's mouth was open. (I didn't see it opening, even though I hadn't broken visual contact with his head. One second it was smiling, and the next it was open as though it were in mid-sentence.)

Then his words came out...

...in the form of a word balloon.

Now, patient reader, you might visualize this in your mind and find it somewhat humorous. I can assure you that it was not. The bizarre balloon was just to the left of his head and the crystal-clear words that were inside it were written in the same all-caps font that comic book text is printed in.

The balloon read, YOU ARE THE STORYTELLER.

As soon as I had finished reading the balloon, it rapidly began fading from sight.

"What?" I muttered, truly confused by this whole thing.

Captain Steel pointed to my chest. His open mouth changed slightly and another balloon appeared to the right of his head displaying the words YOUR NAME IS BOYLE. THE SAME NAME THAT WAS ON THE LIST OF CREATORS. YOU WROTE THE STORIES.

I looked down at where his huge, misshapen hand was pointing. It was the name tag on my suit. "Yes," I said. "I'm John Boyle." Then I took a deep breath of filtered air. "Who are you?"

Another balloon appeared, this time to the left of his proportionately tiny head. It read, I'M CAPTAIN STEEL, TRUE BELIEVER. RIGHTER OF WRONGS. DEFENDER OF PEACE. DON'T YOU RECOGNIZE ME?

I couldn't imagine how frustrating it must have been for this thing to only be able to communicate in this fashion. As soon as I read the last one, it too faded from view. "Mister, I've read Captain Steel. I've pencilled and inked Captain Steel and I've written Captain Steel. You, sir, are no Captain Steel. You've already proven you're not. Now, who the Hell are you?" I still can't believe I said that. It's amazing what can come out of your mouth when you believe your death is a split second away.

The monster's head was suddenly thrust back, in the semblance of hearty laughter. Sure enough, a large balloon soon appeared directly above him which read HA! HA! HAAAA!! in big, bold letters.

My canister of neonite was, unlike those of the rest of the group, swivelled around to my side on my belt because I had been sitting down before Simon and I had taken our little stroll.

Steel's face was now glaring at me again with intense eyes. STORYTELLER, I HAVE GONE BY MANY NAMES. I HAVE HAD MANY TALENTS AND HAD MANY SHORT ADVENTURES ON THIS PLAIN. MY TRUE NAME, HOWEVER, IS QRAVEX. IT WAS THE NAME GIVEN TO ME BY THE UNHOLY ONE ON THE DAY HE PASSED ME THROUGH HIS INFERNAL RECTUM AND MOLDED ME INTO THE THIRD GHACKODEMON.

"The third?"

WHY YES. THIRD OF SIX, TO BE PRECISE. BEZZLEBELLE WAS THE LAST ONE OF US TO COME HERE. THAT WAS IN 1922 AND HERS WAS A PARTICULARLY ENVIABLE EPISODE. WOULD YOU LIKE ME TO TELL YOU OF THE LAST TIME ONE OF MY KIND CAME TO THROUGH THE GRIMOIR'S GATE?

I nodded. I needed the time.

Another balloon formed. A YOUNG MAN HAD FOUND THE GOLDEN GRIMOIR SHORTLY AFTER HIS DEAR SISTER'S UNTIMELY DEATH. THE BITCH HAD BEEN A NUN, YOU SEE, AND SHE HAD DROWNED WHILE SWIMMING A YEAR EARLIER AT THE SUCCULENT AGE OF 22. HAVING LOST FAITH IN THAT SORRY EXCUSE OF A GOD, THE GULLIBLE FUCK TURNED TO US. IT WAS MY TURN TO COME HERE, TO MIDGARD, BUT I DESPISE BEING FEMALE, SO I PASSED UP THE OPPORTUNITY AND

GAVE MY TURN TO BEZZLEBELLE. ONCE HERE, SHE PROCEEDED TO FORNICATE JUST ABOUT EVERY MAN AND BOY SHE COULD WRAP HER SILKY LEGS AROUND. SHE HAD A BALL. SHE HAD LOTS OF BALLS, ACTUALLY. MANY PHOTOGRAPHS WERE TAKEN OF HER GETTING FUCKED SIX WAYS TO SUNDAY WHILE SHE WAS STILL IN HER HABIT. YOU'VE PROBABLY SEEN THEM, RIGHT? AFTER WEEKS OF THIS INDULGENCE, HER BROTHER FINALLY PUT BULLETS IN HER HEAD TO PREVENT ANY FURTHER CONTAMINATION OF HIS TRUE SISTER'S MEMORY. ISN'T THAT A DELIGHTFUL LITTLE TALE, STORYTELLER?

I felt mild shock at his language. Clearly, his original habits and personality were showing through the more he "talked." Either that, or he had been teasing me when he introduced himself as Captain Steel. It was hard to get an impression of his mood because I didn't have the benefit of hearing a voice and that uncertainty was part of what had me shaking.

Another balloon. MY FIRST TIME ON MIDGARD WAS SHORTLY AFTER THE PERFECTION OF THE MECHANICAL CLOCK. I KNOW THIS BECAUSE THE MAN I WAS CRAFTED TO RESEMBLE AND IMITATE WAS A WEALTHY CLOCKMAKER IN ENGLAND. HE HAD DIED OF THE PLAGUE, AS HAD MUCH OF THE POPULATION, AND HIS COMELY YOUNG WIDOW WAS LEFT TO THE COLD AND MERCILESS MACHINATIONS OF THE LOCAL BANK. THE OLD CODGER HAD DIED BEFORE HE COULD SIGN HIS LAST WILL AND TESTAMENT, YOU SEE. THE WIDOW'S PLAN WAS TO HAVE ME SIGN THE WILL BEFORE THE ASSEMBLED BANKERS, THUS ENSURING ITS LEGITIMACY. SHE PERFORMED THE RITUAL AND I CAME. THEN I CAME AGAIN AND AGAIN AND AGAIN.

CHUCKLE IT WAS A RATHER SPLENDID SITUATION. SHE HADN'T CONJURED ME FOR LOVE OR LONGING BUT MERELY FOR GREED. WE HAD OUR NIGHTS TOGETHER BEFORE THE DAY OF THE BANKERS MEETING. SHE PROVIDED ME WITH NOT ONLY HERSELF BUT WITH NEARLY EVERY WHORE IN LONDON. ON THE NIGHT OF THE SIGNING, I STEPPED OUT FROM BEHIND A CURTAIN AND THE MOMENT THOSE OLD BASTARDS SAW ME, THEY PRONOUNCED HER A WITCH AND EXECUTED US BOTH THAT VERY NIGHT. I WASN'T COMPLAINING, THOUGH. I'D GOTTEN **MY** ROCKS OFF.

The release button on the canister of neonite was less than four inches from my arm.

As the last balloon vanished, it was replaced by another. THE NEXT TWO TIMES I CAME HERE, I INDULGED IN MURDER INSTEAD OF THE USUAL PLEASANTRIES. I WAS A BRITISH SOLDIER IN YOUR AMERICAN REVOLUTION. A GENERAL HAD LOST HIS SON DURING THE EARLY PORTION OF THE WAR AND HAD BROUGHT ME HERE OUT OF THE USUAL GRIEF AND PAIN THAT WE ARE SUMMONED TO REMEDY. I ONLY LASTED TWENTY-FOUR HOURS. HIS CAMP WAS ATTACKED BY A RAGTAG AMERICAN MILITIA JUST AS HE WAS FINISHING THE FINAL STAGE OF THE CEREMONY. I MANAGED TO TAKE MANY MEN DOWN WITH ME BEFORE I SUCCUMBED TO THE BLAST OF A CANNON.

NOT TOO LONG AFTER, IT BECAME MY TURN AGAIN. THIS TIME I BECAME THE DAUGHTER OF A FEUDAL LORD IN A LAND CALLED ALABAMA. THIS WAS AN UNSATISFYING TIME AND I SPENT NEARLY A YEAR AS A PRISONER IN THAT MANSION. WOMEN OF THAT CULTURE WERE THINGS TO BE KEPT INDOORS, LIKE

INFANTS. THE PAMPERING GOT OLD, LET ME TELL YOU. THE ONLY PLEASURE I COULD REAP FROM THIS EPISODE WAS AT NIGHT, WHEN I OVERSAW THE TORTURE OF THE NUBIAN SLAVES. THE TASKMASTERS WERE RELUCTANT, AT FIRST, TO ALLOW ME TO VIEW THE MIDNIGHT WHIPPINGS AND CASTRATIONS. BUT WHEN I SHOWED THAT MY ENTHUSIASM FOR INFLICTING HORROR WAS MORE THAN THEIRS, THEY EVENTUALLY BECAME THE SPECTATORS. I DON'T LIKE BEING PENETRATED, YOU SEE. I PREFER TO PENETRATE. TILLY THE IMPALER WAS WHAT THE WRETCHED OVERSEERS BEGAN CALLING ME. THIS LASTED FOR MONTHS. THEN THE NUBIANS STAGED A REVOLT AND SET FIRE TO A PORTION OF THE MANSION. MY PORTION. TILLY THE IMPALER DIED FROM INHALING TOO MUCH SMOKE.

I was mesmerized by his text. He'd been around.

NOW, STORYTELLER, I'VE GIVEN YOU STORIES, YOUR TRADE IN LIFE. NOW YOU WILL PROVIDE ME THAT WHICH I CAME HERE FOR.

I was puzzled. "What?"

I CAN SEE THAT YOU ARE NO FOOL. SO DON'T TRY TO PASS YOURSELF OFF AS ONE.

"I don't know what you mean."

His brow furrowed and his lips curled. For a split second, his impossibly white and shiny teeth became a row of little daggers, like teeth that belonged in a shark's mouth. His blue eyes flashed blood red also. Then he went back to being like before, though still horrific. The hideous Captain Steel. WHEN ONE OF US COMES INTO THIS WORLD WE ATTAIN THE HABITS AND LATENT EMOTIONS OF OUR

TEMPLATES. AS I WAS FLYING ACROSS THE VAST SEA, I HEARD A SOUND. THIS SOUND WAS BARELY AUDIBLE, EVEN TO MY AMAZING EARS. IN ME IT STIRRED THE PREMONITION THAT THE SOURCE OF THIS SOUND WOULD PROVIDE ME WITH PLEASURE. IT WAS A VAGUE PREMONITION... MUCH ABOUT THIS FORM HAS BEEN... **VAGUE**. STORYTELLER, I WANT TO KNOW WHERE THE SOURCE OF THIS SOUND WAS. I DIDN'T SEE A FEMALE WITH YOUR PARTY AS I APPROACHED AND THERE ARE NO OTHER WHELPS FOR MANY MILES. STORYTELLER, IF YOU DO NOT SHARE WITH ME WHAT YOU KNOW OF THIS SOUND, I WILL TEAR YOUR MORTAL SHELL ASUNDER WITH THE SPEED OF A SLOTH!!! If he had said this aloud, the ice beneath me would probably have shook.

"The sound you heard came from a locket. The character that you are currently emulating has a sweetheart named Tenille Trust. In the stories on which your form is based, she calls Captain Steel with this locket."

He closed his eyes, held them shut and then opened them again, looking me in the eye. YOU USED THIS CHARM TO CALL ME HERE. WHY?

"These men wanted to study you."

STUDY ME WITH RIFLES? COME, COME STORYTELLER... THERE WAS MORE TO IT THAN THAT, BUT WE'LL RETURN TO THAT TOPIC IN A MOMENT. BEFORE I KILL YOU, THOUGH, I HAVE MORE QUESTIONS ABOUT THIS BODY.

"All your questions could have been answered by those people you killed in New York, the ID Comics staff"

THAT WAS A HASTY ACT. I WAS PISSED OFF.

"Why?"

WHY?? ISN'T IT **OBVIOUS**???

I shook my head, dumbfounded. He was a horny entity, this was obvious. A being of his power would have no problem taking women by force.

But he hadn't done so.

I WAITED NEARLY 80 YEARS FOR MY NEXT MIDGARD ADVENTURE. THE GRIMOIR FELL INTO THE HANDS OF A GROUP OF YOUTHS WHO DIDN'T EVEN KNOW WHAT THEY HAD. THEN THEY ALL KILLED THEMSELVES IN A RIDICULOUS SHOWING OF APPRECIATION TOWARD HIS LUGUBRIOUSNESS. ALL SAVE ONE, THAT IS, AND HE WAS AN **IDIOT**. A WAIF. AN OBSEQUIOUS PIECE OF FLOTSAM WHO HAD NOT EXPERIENCED ONE TENTH OF WHAT A MAN HIS AGE SHOULD HAVE. I LISTENED TO HIS DREAMS AND FOUND THAT HE HAD SEVERAL COLORFUL FRIENDS WHOM HE HAD NOT SEEN IN SOME TIME. **POWERFUL** FRIENDS. HIS GREATEST FRIEND WAS A HERO CALLED CAPTAIN STEEL. I CAREFULLY SUGGESTED TO THE IDIOT THAT HE READ THE BOOK. HE DID SO AND AS HE DID, I WAS ABLE TO SEE INTO HIS MIND MORE AND MORE CLEARLY. HIS FRIENDS WERE VIRTUAL **GODS**! THEY HAD POWER. THEY HAD PRESTIGE. IN SOME CASES, THEY HAD WEALTH. MY GHACKODAEMON BRETHREN DOUBTED THAT SUCH BEINGS EXISTED ON THIS PLAIN, BUT I WAS CONVINCED BY THE PASSION AND WHOLE-HEARTED CONFIDENCE THE BOY HAD THAT THEY WERE GENUINE. IT NEVER EVEN OCCURRED TO ME THAT THE MAN-BOY WAS MAD! ON THE NIGHT OF MY RECREATION, I STEPPED THROUGH THE PORTAL AND IMMEDIATELY FELL TO THE GROUND. I HAD FALLEN BECAUSE THESE LEGS OF MINE WERE SO HORRIBLY

MISSHAPEN THAT I COULDN'T WALK OR EVEN STAND.
THE BODY WAS AN ABOMINATION! IT DIDN'T EVEN
LOOK **REAL**! THE CRETIN INFORMED ME THAT I COULD
LEVITATE AND SO I DID. I THEN ASKED HIM TO SHOW
ME PICTURES AND BIOGRAPHICAL INFORMATION ON
CAPTAIN STEEL. THESE THINGS ARE NEEDED IN ORDER
TO PERFORM THE CEREMONY. WHAT HE HANDED ME
WAS A FLIMSY CHILDREN'S PAMPHLET FEATURING A
RIDICULOUS CARICATURE AS THE MAIN CHARACTER. I
HAD BEEN DUPED!!

Sex was the central preoccupation of these
creatures. They came to Earth. They screwed their
brains out. They departed.

THEN I LOOKED DOWN AND SAW THAT I WAS
NEUTER! NEUTER!!! IN MY UNMATCHED RAGE, I
LASHED OUT AT THAT PITIFUL FLEA. HE WAS A LAZY
THING. HE NEVER DID ANYTHING EXCEPT READ
CHILDREN'S DREK AND WATCH THAT GLOWING BOX IN
THE CORNER. SO, I DECIDED TO GIVE HIM A REASON
FOR THIS. I'M WILLING TO BET THAT HIS LIFESTYLE
HASN'T CHANGED ONE IOTA!!

I looked at him more closely. His skin was the
same texture as his costume. His costume was his
skin. Qravex couldn't take it off because Captain
Steel hadn't taken it off in the comic book that
Timmy had used.

"Why did you destroy monuments?"

WHY NOT? DAEMONS OF ALL TYPES SEEK TO
DESTROY BEAUTY. THE GHACKODAEMONS SPECIALIZE
IN DESTROYING THE REPUTATIONS OF THOSE WHOM WE
ARE SUMMONED TO REPLACE. DESTROYING THE
VARIOUS SYMBOLS OF MAN'S MINUSCULE
ACHIEVEMENTS WAS ONE OF THE WAYS IN WHICH I

ACCOMPLISHED THIS. BUT THEN, THIS FORM ISN'T REALLY ALL THAT BENEVOLENT IS IT, STORYTELLER?

"What do you mean?"

I MEAN THAT THIS "CAPTAIN STEEL" ISN'T REALLY A PROTAGONIST AT ALL. HE'S PART OF THE GREAT DECEPTION. THE SATISFACTION OF TARNISHING AND RUINING A REPUTATION... EVEN **THAT** WAS DENIED ME THIS TIME. NOT ONLY WAS THIS HERO NOT REAL TO BEGIN WITH, BUT HE WAS ON THE SIDE OF SATAN FROM THE VERY BEGINNING. ALL "SUPERHEROES" ARE. DIDN'T YOU KNOW THAT?

I shook my head.

THEIR FLASHY FABLES ARE MEANT TO DIVERT THE ATTENTION OF CHILDREN AWAY FROM THE PROPHETS OF THE SO-CALLED "ALMIGHTY" AND HIS BRATLING. YOU KNOW THIS TO BE TRUE! THE CHILDREN OF THIS WORLD ARE MORE FAMILIAR WITH THE ADVENTURES OF CAPTAIN STEEL THAN THEY ARE WITH THE STORIES OF THE CHRIST CHILD!! HA! HA!! HAAAA!!!

I must confess to having been horrified by this revelation. Still am. He was from Hell and not to be trusted, but his words had the ring of truth in them.

Qravex's head was suddenly thrust back again, as though he were shouting at the sky. THIS SHELL IS NUMB! IT DOESN'T FEEL COLD OR HOT OR PLEASURE OR PAIN OR ANYTHING!! IT'S DRIVING ME INSANE!! IT'S WORSE THAN BEING IN LIMBO!!! Then he brought his head forward again and glared at me. AND THE WORST PART IS, I DON'T THINK I CAN GO BACK! STORYTELLER, TELL ME THAT THERE IS A WAY. TELL ME THAT THIS BODY CAN DIE AND THAT I CAN GO BACK TO MY REALM AND AWAIT MY NEXT TURN!!

I couldn't resist. "Captain Steel is invulnerable. You must have discovered that by now."

SEVEN HELLS... NOOOOO!!!!!!!

Even though his words were not spoken with a voice, they rumbled right through me.

I CANNOT ENDURE **THIS**!! Tears were running down his grotesque face now. HOW LONG WILL IT TAKE BEFORE THIS THING DIES OF OLD AGE?

"He's immortal," I said with a grin.

The entity was bewildered. He levitated backwards as if staggering. Then he seemed to regain some of his composure. YOU'RE **LYING**! I'M AN EXPERT AT THAT. EVERY GOD HAS A RAGNAROK! EVERY ACHILLES HAS A HEEL!

I'm thinking now that I must have been a little drunk on the power I had to make him distressed.

It was then that I noticed something else above his head. It was another balloon, only different from the ones that he used to speak. It was shaped like a cartoon cloud. A thought balloon. It was only there for an instant, like those little strands of hair and debris that you see on a movie screen. A flash. But it was long enough.

The thought balloon contained just three words, JUST KILL HIM.

I was in a hopeless situation. It had nothing to lose by killing me. My moment of clarity probably saved my life. My voice cracked as I came up with a glimmer of hope for him. "All right. I'll help you on your way. But it won't be pleasant."

DO IT, MAN! HURRY! QRAVEX BEGS YOU!!

I grabbed the canister and actuated the mechanism. Captain Steel/Qravex fell to the ground instantly, bathed in purple light. He curled in the fetal position and his word balloons began to display mostly long strings of vowels. A few of them said things like I-I-IT'S C-COLD and another said IT BURNS! I'M BEING DISEMBOWELED!! His thought balloons were becoming more visible now as well. The ones I could make out appeared to contain verses, probably from some sort of dark Lord's Prayer. I placed the canister on the ground next to him and walked over to my dead team. Having collected their canisters, I systematically kept Qravex's exposure constant. I didn't bother reading his words.

I just waited.

I waited for fifteen minutes.

Then I felt something hot on my shoulder. I turned and saw that my suit was burning there. I turned to see the smiling green eyes of Captain Steel. I reached for my sidearm and drew it. Then I got right down close to him and put the barrel to one of his eyes and pulled the trigger. The kick surprised me. The bullet went right through his eye socket and out the back of his head with a nice, wet, muffled popping sound.

A small balloon appeared next to his mouth. I tried not to look at it, but I did. I'LL BE WAITING FOR YOU, STORYTELLER... IN... HIS... BOWELS....

I put the barrel up to his other eye and repeated the procedure. He didn't make any more balloons after that. At the very end, he dissolved into a green goo that then rapidly dried up and blew away.

For the last few paragraphs, I've been fighting the need to puke.

My hair is falling out now. It landed on my hands and keyboard in small wisps just a few seconds ago as I was telling you how the monster died. A big clump of it just came out as I rubbed my crown.

And it's grey.

The End.

THE MUSCLEBOUND BOYS
By Darin Wagner

The hulking Dean of Admissions shook his head as he returned to his desk. "I'm sorry young one, but I'm afraid you do not meet our qualification requirements."

The 25-year-old applicant shifted forward in his chair and stared deeply into the older man's eyes for a moment and then asked, "Sir, in what way do I not meet your requirements?"

The Dean's eyes grew wide for a split-second, as though they had momentarily met those of an animal. He regained his composure a heartbeat later and straightened his back. "W-well your academic record is exemplary of course. Valedictorian of Bearclaw High School, Alaska, Class of '51. Your psychological profile *reads* stable and you have a projected professional success factor of six point eight."

"So what's the problem, sir?"

"Well, as you know, this institution prides itself on the sheer *perfection* of its students. We, here at Spumco University, have a near-ancient tradition of excellence in cultivating the minds and *bodies* of our students. And while your academic record is superb, I'm afraid your athletic record seems to be more than a little questionable."

The young man shifted back in his chair to his former position. "My *athletic* record?"

"Come come now... your high school may have been fooled by these ersatz logs and records, but *not* this university." The Dean spun his desk terminal around on its swivel so that the boy could see the screen. "These are clearly forgeries. Clever forgeries, but forgeries nonetheless. And the more I read between the lines and into your *real* athletic record, the more Enronic it becomes. Each section, upon my close examination, reveals that you've disregarded federal student requirements. I have to wonder why you even bothered to apply here, son/lad. These transcripts show evidence that, for the seven-year duration of your high school education, you neglected to go to body-building practice. That kind of acedia is simply not what higher education is all about."

"'Practice?' The people who call it that don't know the meaning of the word," the boy-of-25 shot back. "Lying in a bed for an hour with lines connected to you, getting your muscles buzzed… it's useless."

The Dean's eyebrows collided. "It's hardly 'useless.' Without the electrolysis treatments, most people would go into atrophy. That's why body-building became a mandatory part of the education system almost ninety years ago. And I'm sure you're aware, it's also a mandatory part of any employment package and health care plan."

"Do I look like I'm suffering from muscle atrophy?" the boy-of-25 asked as he rose from his chair to his full height of 5'9".

The Dean responded by rising from *his* chair to his full 6'8" height and flexed his pectoral muscles, stretching his shirt nearly to the point of tearing.

"Son/lad, you are surprisingly well toned, but you don't look like myself or most of the students on this campus, or even most retirement home residents. I mean, *look* at you."

"What about me?"

The Dean ran his fingers through his artificially blackened hair as if searching there for his answer. Then his eyes lit up. "Windows, are you online?" he called out.

The computer system that was all around them (and hiding behind majestic, antique-filled mahogany shelves) came to life and answered in one of the 90 different female voices that came with the latest version, "Affirmation. I am always online."

"Good," said the Dean. "Tell me, what is this applicant's body fat percentage?"

The familiar Megasoft chime sounded as the request for data was acknowledged. Three seconds later, the machine replied, "11%."

"Thank you, Windows. Now then... the average male student at this university has a body fat percentage of 3%. The highest I believe we've had in the last four decades has been 5%. That one was expelled."

"And this is consequential... how?"

"You know why. It is a recognized standard that we have consistently maintained. No university in the *worlds* would settle for anything greater than 7% body fat. Why, the average 56-year-old has less proportionate body fat than you do. I can't fathom how you can tolerate being in such deplorable shape, personally."

"Actually, I'm in excellent shape, sir," the boy declared with confidence.

"By whose standards?" the Dean demanded half-heartedly.

"Indeed."

"This is pointless, young man. There's nothing you can say that will alter the fact that you are unfit for this or any other university in our system. We don't admit heteroclites. Now, perhaps if you adopted the proper body-building regiment, you can achieve an acceptable height-weight-body fat ratio before--"

"Sir, I can out-perform your star athlete," said the boy, again with self-assuredness.

That was the funniest thing the 6'8" Dean of Admissions had heard in some time and he responded by casually stripped off his shirt and tie, revealing a massive display of muscle and veins. Amidst poorly restrained snickering he asked, "Would you be so good as to remove your own shirt and tie for a moment, applicant?"

The boy complied.

"Now then, I'm 42-years-old and my muscles are cold right now. Examinate." The Dean then boldly struck one of the more celebrated poses in the sport of body building. "Even though I'm not pumped, it's still pretty obvious that I'm physically superior to you, and again I'm 42-years-old. Now, how do you think you'd compare to Jet Osborne?"

Jet Osborne was a senior and the reigning campus bodybuilding champion.

"Sir, what do your athletes *do*?"

"I'm afraid I don't understand your question, applicant."

"What do they do all day?"

The Dean sighed. "I'm afraid you will have to define 'do.'"

"Before I went to high school, I found a diary. A journal, belonging to an ancestor of mine. From back when there was just Urth, and before anything man-made ever left it."

"Computers haven't been around that long!" the Dean snapped.

"It wasn't e-lit, it was a *book*. It was handwritten, on paper. In it my ancestor wrote of working on his family farm and of exercising in the off-seasons. Swimming. Wrestling with the other boys in his social tier and fighting for honor amongst his peers. He *ran*. He didn't just take cardio-vascular enhancers and sit through electrolysis treatments. You see, he *used* his body... his muscles. They weren't just used to get him from shuttle-to-shuttle and seat-to-seat. They weren't just something to look at. He relied on them. He built structures with primitive tools, powered by his own body. He did things called 'push-ups' and 'chin-ups', even when he didn't have to, and he endured the discomfort of doing them. He also often spoke of the virtue of work, and how it accelerated the maturing process and--"

The Dean's nose was arched into an extreme sneer. "'Swimming?'" he interrupted. "That's what fish do, applicant. 'Wrestling?' Bears and troglosaurs do that sort of thing. Humans do not. We *think*. What you're talking about is sheer arctoid bestiality."

The calm boy looked at the older man with a measured and tempered gaze. "Are you saying that humans can't do something as simple as swim or fight?"

"Why of course we can! But such things are totally unnecessary, not to mention absolutely beneath us. Robots do our fighting. U-cars take us underwater if that's where we want to go. For a person to do these things unaided is a waste of time and it's an even bigger waste of time to rehearse these activities for no reason. And all this business about physical exertion being better for you than electrolysis is pure postoffice! Is this what you've been supplementing your electrolysis treatments with? Menial *labor*? 'Working out' as you call it? And that last bit of insanity... How can simple muscular locomotion possibly affect one's mind? Maturity comes with acquisition of information! Absorbing and retaining data!" The Dean was too upset to realize that the applicant didn't have to be in his office anymore. "Windows, does electrolysis produce more muscle mass in humans than a regular regiment of physical exertion?"

The surrounding computer once again chimed from behind framed artwork and antique George Foreman Grills and reported, "Affirmation. In order for an average human to achieve the same proportionate muscle mass through physical exertion as he or she would through electrolysis, said person would have to do such menial exercise movements for a minimum of two hours a day instead of only one hour of electrolysis per day. This would also need to be done in conjunction with a radically different nutritional regiment that would involve less variety. The results would also vary drastically from person-to-person. Most would not achieve the same high level of muscle-mass and low body fat percentage that they could with electrolysis combined with fat neutralizers, cardio-vascular enhancers and other techniques."

"Does 'more muscle-mass' mean 'stronger?' Does it mean 'faster?'" the boy blurted out at the Dean's office computer.

Windows chimed again, though this time in a set of minor keys, and said, "Affirmation. By definition, muscles are responsible for strength. Therefore, more muscle mass equals more strength. Since muscles are also responsible for locomotion, more muscle-mass also equals more speed, should the unlikely event occur that someone would need to move unaided at an accelerated velocity."

A lowly applicant speaking to the Dean's own computer was not something he was accustomed to at all and the Dean quickly reasserted dominion over his database. "Windows, does physical use of the muscles of the human body factor in any way with the speed at which one matures mentally?"

Windows replied, "There is no scientific or political support for the statement that excessive use of a human's muscle groups in a manual fashion promotes mental or psychological development."

"And there you have it," said the Dean, reaching for his shirt.

The boy was stone. "I can physically overpower you, sir."

"I'm afraid I don't respond well to empty threats or hasty attempts at humor," the Dean said, chuckling.

"That was neither, sir… but I am giving you the opportunity to change my whole world view."

"All right, young fool. If you can somehow manage to physically overpower me using your pathetic musculature, I will give your file "approved" status. *When* you fail, I want you out of my office. Agreed?"

"Agreed."

The boy-who-was-25 had Windows describe a primitive contest to the still-chiding Dean. When both men were ready, the two of them locked up, hands in the air above their heads with fingers laced. The two men struggled against each other. When he thought he'd waited long enough, the boy brought the Dean of Admissions to his knees at will. As his gloriously picturesque physique failed him and the discomfort of being forced to the floor shot through his nervous system, the Dean cried out. The boy let go and the Dean sat on the floor with his legs out and his back hunched. Then the Dean began to whine and pout... just as he had done all his life whenever things didn't go his way.

Wesley
By Darin Wagner

Friday February 12

    I was given a new job today just before I left for home. Apparently, Ken Phillips over at St. Pius Elementary School has rather suddenly resigned. Until they can get a replacement counselor, I'm going to be taking over his responsibilities over there in addition to my own as counselor here at the St. Pius High School. "Shouldn't be too difficult," Sister Marsha told me over the phone. She's the principal over there. The children are apparently very well-mannered and adjusted, so much so that Phillips' work load was light enough for him to teach Math to the sixth graders on the side.

    Evidently, it wasn't his work load that prompted his resignation. The only real task he had that was out of the ordinary so far this year was a fighting incident that occurred on the playground at recess yesterday involving two boys; 5th grader Chad Basski, 11, and 2nd grader Wesley Bova, 7. Hardly an even match. There was an ambulance involved, I'm told. I'll find out more on Monday. I'll be spending my mornings at the High School and then, after lunch, I'll be crossing the athletic field and spending the rest of the day at the Elementary. I hope they can get a new student counselor before the end of the year. I don't like the Elementary very much. It looks like an old, Charles Dickens factory with crosses on it. I can't believe the thing still meets code.

Monday, February 15

I arrived at the Elementary today during a recess period and Sister Marsha greeted me a the door. She said that she'd taken it upon herself to assist the playground monitors after what had transpired last Thursday. Sister Marsha isn't like the other four nuns who still work at the Elementary, by the way. She doesn't wear a habit. She wears a wig and a dress with a blouse straight from the fifties. The other nuns all wear those neo-habit get-ups. I tried not to stare at the golden brackets that hold her teeth, most of them rotten, in place. She took me to her office and showed me school portraits of the two boys. Chad Basski's dad is a local plumber, she informed me, and donated much of his time to the Elementary's most recent renovation, among other things. Chad was the third Basski child to attend the St. Pius parish school system, just like their father had. They were prominent members of the parish. Wesley Bova's parents had moved to town four years ago with their toddler and bought one of the local restaurants, The Coffee Cup Cafe. Wesley is the only child. I asked about the fight and how severe Wesley had been beaten. Sister Marsha's face went slack and with a look of cold seriousness she informed me that it was *Chad*, not Wesley, who had been rushed to the hospital. Chad was found by the aids lying unconscious on the paved section of the playground next to the dumpsters. Examinations taken later had shown that Chad suffered two injuries; a severely bruised sternum and a blow to the back of the head. I asked her what Wesley had hit him with. She said that the other children had stated that Wesley had "kicked him." He apparently "kicked" Chad squarely in the chest, which in turn had caused Chad to bang his head on the dumpster. I said the children must be lying. There is no way, I told her, that a 2nd grader could kick a 5th grader like that and do that kind of damage. Most kids Wesley's age couldn't get their foot up high enough to meet a 5th grader's sternum, unless the 5th grader is on his knees and that didn't match the witness accounts. Chad's parents agree with me, she said. They remain convinced that it was some sort of accident. Chad claims not to be able to recall the incident.

      I asked Sister Marsha to take me around so I could get a look at the boys, among other things. I'm still pretty new to the parish schools and I'd only seen the Elementary briefly before. We went to Chad's class first. Peering at the classroom from the hall, behind the glass window of the door, Sister Marsha and I could see him struggling to pay attention. The back of his head had a bandage on it and so did his chest, under his sweater. He looked like a trouble maker, big for his age. Then she took me two floors up and showed me Wesley. He is about half Chad's height. I continued to assert that there had to have been more to the situation than was being told. Sister Marsha agreed and then took me to Phillips' old office. Phillips was also a prominent member of the parish until this week. There's a "For Sale" sign up in the Phillips family's front yard.

While rooting through Phillips' paperwork, I found his notes concerning what the playground aids said the witnesses had seen. (Here say. Gotta love it. It's been my experience that *here say* is usually good enough for nuns.) They all said the same thing. Chad was taunting Wesley. Chad shoved Wesley. Wesley hauled off and kicked Chad, knocking him back into the dumpster.

Chad's record lists him at 110 lbs. Wesley weighs 60 lbs.

Something doesn't add up. Most seven-year-olds can't hit or kick well, no matter how many times they've seen *Rocky III* or *Enter The Dragon*. They're just not coordinated enough at that age. So they shove rather than hit, usually. Also, most boys at these ages are under the impression that only "sissies" and/or girls kick. Wesley isn't, according to his record, much of an athlete. At 2nd grade, he hasn't done much more than play dodgeball in Phy Ed.. Chad is on the youth wrestling team and got third place at State.

It must have been a fluke.

Wednesday, January 17

Wesley Bova uttered profanity at Sister Geneva, the school librarian, today. This occurred during my dental appointment this afternoon and so the matter was dealt with by Sister Marsha. I've scheduled a meeting with him for tomorrow afternoon. In the meantime, he's been assigned both a penance to write (500 words, kind of harsh for a 2nd grader if you ask me) as well as an apology to give to Sister Geneva. His parents have also been notified.

In other news, freshman Randy Kirby was caught cheating on a Geography test. The Monsignor decided that he should wash and wax the floor of the chapel after school. He asked me for my opinion and I told him that was fine.

Tonight, I had a meeting with concerned parents pertaining to an upcoming Sadie Hawkins Dance that was proposed by the high school senior student council. Roughly half of the parents seemed to fear that the nature of the girls-ask-boys dance would influence their daughters to become promiscuous or compel them to become prostitutes later in life. I felt like telling them that this is the 1980s and not the 1880s. One mother even asked why high school dances had to be co-ed! I was momentarily silent, waiting for some indication that she was making a joke. When she gave no such indication, I told her, "So that your kids don't grow up to be homosexual." She believed me.

Thursday, January 18

Suffice it to say, I was totally unprepared for my meeting with Wes Bova. Oh, I *thought* I was prepared. I read his file and talked to a couple of his teachers before the meeting, but it is evident to me now that all that was ineffective. I might as well start with what I read and heard before the meeting:

Wes was a satisfactory student until two weeks ago. His quarterly evaluations all said the usual cookie-cutter things such as "your son shows great potential" and "is very well behaved." That line about potential is standard. All kids get that on their report cards until junior high. There's no alternative, really. (Imagine what kind of fury would be wrought if a report card read "your son shows absolutely no potential whatsoever." But I digress.) Two weeks ago, however, Wes became *super*-satisfactory. His Math and Language Arts grades all showed a dramatic improvement. In fact, beginning two weeks ago, he hasn't answered a single question incorrectly on an assignment or test.

His Homeroom, Math, Language Arts and Phy Ed teachers all had some rather interesting things to say to me. Wes wasn't just acing his tests, he was finishing them at a breakneck pace. Typical Math tests allowed a half an hour. Less than three minutes after a teacher would say "begin," Wes was waltzing up to the desk and turning in his test. One teacher told him that he needed to take the test back to his desk and take it more seriously. Wes, she said, replied by winking at her and turning it in right then and there anyway. After two days of this, his teachers began trying to look over his shoulder to see if they could catch him cheating. At first, they couldn't get from the front of the room to his desk inconspicuously in time before he was finished. One teacher decided to move him to the front of the classroom so that she could. She said that when she said "begin," Wes filled out the twenty-five question test as though it were a voting ballot and he was a die-hard Republican or Democrat. "Boom, boom, boom, done! Just like that" was what she said. His Phy Ed teacher (Glen Karr) had different things to say, given the nature of his class. He said that Wes suddenly dominated the dodgeball games. Before, he was usually picked last for teams. (I hate that, by the way. That is <u>no way</u> to treat a child's self esteem.) But since he started "kicking ass," he's been picked first. One day, the class had to climb a rope to the ceiling of the gym. Or at least try to. Wes watched the other kids and their attempts. Three of the other kids made it to the top. Wes did too, only he didn't use his legs. "He was possessed," said Mr. Karr. "I've never seen that level of focus and determination in a second grader... or even an *eighth* grader. Can't wait till he's old enough for football!" I asked Mr. Karr if it were even possible for a little boy to climb a hemp rope some 35 feet into the air with just his arms. He replied, "Sure, but it must have hurt like Hell. He was probably sore all day." If Wes was sore, he didn't mention it to anyone, even his parents.

At this point, two things seemed certain; first, I was about to have a meeting with a very smart 2nd grader and second, he was out to prove something. His records prior to two weeks ago indicated that he was an introverted child. Not out-going. Not aggressive. Two of the kids that he did play with at recess from time-to-time said that he got pushed around and verbally abused by Chad Basski quite a bit on the playground on a regular basis. Chad had apparently figured out how to do so without attracting the attention of the playground aids (who are church volunteers, I might add, with no professional training in dealing with children).

Wes Bova walked into my office and I asked him to have a seat. He sat down like an aristocrat getting ready to view an opera. He then patiently waited for me to begin. I could already tell something was not right. Most children are nervous and fidgety when they know that they are in trouble or when meeting a new authority figure. Wes was neither nervous nor fidgety. He was serene and calm. Relaxed. In retrospect, I think he may actually have been *bored* and was purposely trying not to give the impression of being interested out of a sense of respect and/or politeness towards me. Our meeting was brief. I had intended to let it be longer, but after a few short minutes and a few short exchanges back and forth, I wanted him to leave my office. Immediately. He hadn't said or done anything wrong, but he definitely said and did things that were not right.

First of all, he was very patient. Not like a well-behaved little boy. No, this was different. I asked him how he was feeling today. What I expected to hear was "fine." (That's one of the child world's favorite descriptive words. They invariably use it to describe themselves. They use the word "nice" to describe just about everything else. It gets annoying, believe me.) But what Wes said was "splendid." I began lecturing to him about the necessity to conform to the school's rules of conduct. I didn't bother invoking Christian morals into my little micro-lecture, since I figured Sister Marcia had already delivered those messages to him in spades. Most of the words that I was using were quite big, I now realize. Too big for a 2nd grader to understand. I was still in "high school mode," you see. But he got every word of it, I'm sure of that. He was genuinely listening to what I was saying and wasn't giving me that dull, trance-like stare little boys usually project in that kind of situation. But that wasn't all he was doing. He was also studying me. Searching for weaknesses.

I have to get this out right here and right now. His eyes were what made me want to get him out of there. The human eye stays pretty much the same in size from childhood to adulthood. This is why children often appear to have such huge irises and pupils. It's because, proportionately, they do. It's that wide-eyed look of wonder that delights grandparents and saps the will of liberal parents. Wes didn't have that wide-eyed look. The look he was giving me was one that I haven't seen even in any of my high school students. It was mature. It was authoritarian. The last time I saw a look like that, it was when I was looking up at a cop who had pulled me over for speeding. Wes was projecting an adult look at me from eyes that were too big for his head. I stammered and stopped in mid-sentence and we stared for what must have been five to ten seconds.

He isn't a little boy. That's what his eyes told me, anyway.

I regained my composure and finished the lecture, but I didn't maintain eye-contact with him for very long. I could see in my peripheral vision that he had a smirk. I asked him to produce his penance and he did and handed it to me. He looked like a midget car salesman (or an imp) handing me a contract. Before I sent him back to class, I asked him two questions. The first was, "Why did you call Sister Geneva what you did?" To which he smiled answered with the theatrically blatant lie, "I don't know." I blurted out my next question rather clumsily. It was "Where did you learn to kick?" He paused on his way out the door and then turned to me and answered, "Bud's."

After he had left, I "sobered up" (so-to-speak) and then called his parents, both of whom were at The Coffee Cup. I asked if I could meet with them for a late breakfast tomorrow morning and they agreed.

I've decided to keep an eye on that young man.

Friday, January 19

My late breakfast with the Bovas at their cafe didn't shed much light on their son's recent and drastic change in behavior, but I did learn a couple of things. First, both parents were just as surprised by Wes's "fight" with Chad Basski as his teachers were. And second, they too, have seen a difference in their son's behavior, though it is hardly a red-flag raising difference. They said that he has gotten more respectful and obedient these last couple of weeks. He's actually keeping his room clean and doesn't have to be told to do hardly anything anymore. And if they do tell him to do something, they only have to do so once and that is all. He had usually watched cartoons after school, but now he's coming over to The Coffee Cup to help them clean and close for the day every day after school.

I'm pretty confused by this. He injures another student on the playground and he tells off a nun at his school... *but*... he's blowing everybody away academically and he's treating his parents like royalty. This doesn't follow any of the established patterns of any psychological condition so far documented in any of my books. I don't think he's being abused. I don't think his parents are anything out-of-the-ordinary.

Just before I left The Coffee Cup Cafe, I asked them if he hangs around anyone named "Bud." Mr. Bova said no. I asked if they knew anyone at all named "Bud." They said no, initially. Then Mrs. Bova off-handedly mentioned that she had an uncle named Bud who was a dairy farmer in Minnesota. I asked how often they see Uncle Bud. Her voice lowered and she told me that Uncle Bud died in a tractor pull contest when she was a little girl. When they asked me why I asked, I told them about what Wes had told me at our meeting yesterday and that they should be on the lookout for anybody named "Bud."

Nothing out-of-the-ordinary happened at the school today, other than Sally Peterson losing one of her front baby teeth. She was sobbing because she was convinced that her mother would be mad at her for losing the tooth. She thought she lost it because she ate too much candy and didn't brush enough. I had to assure her that this was normal and not a result of bad oral hygiene. Telling her that it was okay really made me feel good.

Monday, January 22

An uneventful day at both schools.

Tuesday, January 23

Fire alarm drills were conducted today at the Elementary. All went according to plan, but there was one minor story that I got from one of the teachers concerning Wes. During the drill, one of the fifth graders was horsing around and accidentally knocked a fire extinguisher out of it's cabinet. The seal on it broke and was making a hissing sound. One of the teachers remarked that it was going to make a mess. Wes corrected her by telling her that the extinguisher in question was a "CO2" extinguisher and that she was thinking of an "A Triple F" extinguisher. He went on to say that the CO2 extinguisher released no solid material, only cold gas. When she asked him what an "A Triple F" extinguisher had in it, he told her that "A Triple F" was an acronym that stood for "Aqueous Film Forming Foam." If any other child had said this, I would assume it was something that he/she had remembered from watching television or overhearing their parents. Wes's parents do own a cafe, after all, and they are required to keep extinguishers of specific types. Still...

Wednesday, January 24

Another uneventful day for me.

Thursday, January 25

Wes got his first incorrect answer on a test in almost three weeks today and it was a puzzling answer at that. The question was multiple choice and asked "Who is our State Governor?" The choices were

     A. Tony Earl
     B. Earl Tony
     C. Ronald Reagan
     D. None of the above

The answer, of course, is "A" but Wes answered with "D." When his teacher showed him the error, Wes just shrugged his shoulders, as though it was no big deal, and said, "I couldn't remember." This is odd for two reasons. First, this was a review of information learned at the beginning of the quarter... prior, however, to Wes's unexplained increase in academic performance. Second, if he's so dedicated to his tests and assignments and their perfection, I would have thought that he would have exhibited more concern over the missed answer.

Friday, January 26

I've re-written this entry twice already. I still don't know where to begin, except to say that what I saw and heard today has got me so upset that I won't be able to sleep tonight, regardless of what I take. It involved, of course, Wes Bova.

While I was making my way across the athletic field for my Elementary afternoon, Wes got into trouble again. This time it was with Mr. Karr in Phy Ed.. Wes was not paying attention as Mr. Karr was explaining the rules of horse to the class and so Karr took him aside for a disciplinary chat. Wes called him a "pot-smoking shit pigeon" to his face.

Karr immediately called down for Sister Marcia and she was escorting him to her office when I entered the hallway right behind them without being noticed. I was right behind the two of them and saw the whole thing.

Sister Marsha was telling him things about God and about respect and more things about God and, when his body language indicated that he wasn't listening, she grabbed his ear for leverage. Wes reached up to the hand that had him by the ear and broke her pinky finger with a twist. Then he further took advantage of her momentary shock and pain and twisted the arm back and broke her elbow. The sound of the finger breaking was bad, but the noise from her elbow made me freeze, then wince. She was in so much pain she couldn't shout or scream. She sobbed to God in a hoarse voice as she slid down the wall into a sitting position clasping her twisted arm. It was bizarre. It was quick. His movements were almost poetic in their expression. He then whispered something in her ear and that was when I came out of my trance and ran up to the fainting Sister Marcia and told her I was calling for an ambulance. She was muttering things about Lucifer as she was going under. I then told Wes to go to my office and stay there until I got back. My voice cracked when I did so. A couple of teachers poked their heads out of their classes and then came running. We had to help the First Responders get Sister Marcia onto the stretcher.

After she was taken to the hospital, I went back to my office and sat down at my desk in front of the little man. He was calm. What had just happened was clearly no big deal to him. I reached under my desk and activated the video recorder in the wall. He then informed me that the camera was broken. I turned and, sure enough, the lense on the camera mounted in the upper corner of the room was visibly broken. Something broke it. I turned back to him and demanded to know how it happened. He batted his eyes at me as if to say, "How would *I* know?"

We stared at each other for what felt like two or three minutes. In his eyes, I saw a range of emotions. Complex emotions that no child his age should have, according to Spock and other experts. His gaze never relented.

I relented. I asked him who he was. He said he was "Wesley Dean Bova" with a smile. I asked him what he wanted. He said, "Nothing." I then suggested that he tell me exactly what was going on. He asked me what I meant. I told him that he didn't have to play dumb in here. I told him that, in my office, he can be himself and that he didn't have to pretend to be like the other children in his class. I also told him that he probably *wanted* to stop pretending, even if just for a little while. At that point, all pretenses were dropped and I saw him change. It wasn't actually physical, but it seemed just like he had removed a mask. What lied underneath said mask was definitely not a seven year old boy. I then said, "that's better" and asked him why he kicked Chad Basski on the playground. With remarkable relaxation and self-assuredness, he said "He left me few options. He wasn't treating me with respect."
"Fair enough," I said. Then I asked him why he had called Sister Geneva, the librarian, "a big bull dike." He replied, "Because she is." I asked him how he

knew that. He said that it was "common knowledge" where he comes from. I asked him where he comes from and he just smiled back at me. I asked him why his grades have gone up to nearly perfect in the last three weeks. He said that they'd "always been that way." I pulled out his report card and showed him that, in fact, they hadn't always been that way and he said someone must have made a mistake with his records. I told him that something like that was unlikely. That was when he jumped up onto my desk faster than I could move and rested on his haunches in front of me and got right up into my face and whispered, "Listen, you infinitesimal little bureaucratic bookworm bitch, don't *fuck* with me. If I'm capable of breaking an old woman's arm, then I'm more than capable of doing worse to *your* piddley ass." He paused for effect and then said, "There. Is. Nothing. Wrong. With. Me. Now let's here you say that."

"If you want people to think there is nothing wrong with you then you need to stop doing things that little boys don't or shouldn't know how to do," I whispered back. "Little boys don't send people to the hospital twice a month and they don't talk like you do." He was still staring into my eyes, trying to freak me out (and being somewhat successful), but he was also assessing my statement. "Is it 'common knowledge' where you come from that Mr. Karr is a pot-smoker, too?" I asked.

He said, "Oh yes. He'll lose his job because of it and he'll turn into the village junky, in addition to already being the village idiot. Just give him six more years."

I asked him what he said to Sister Marcia after he broke her arm. He said, "I told her that if she ever touched my ears again, I'd cut her's off and wear them around my neck. Anything else, you'd like to know?"

The last thing I asked him before he hopped back down off of my desk was, "What did you say to Mr. Phillips on his last day, during your meeting with him that afternoon?"

He grinned and said, "I believe my exact words were, 'Jesus Christ, Ken! I mean, your own *niece*? She's only, what? Five years old?'"

Saturday, January 28

While Wes had somehow managed to wreck the lense on the camera in my office, he hadn't managed to sabotage the microphone. It was the audio from my meeting with him (excluding the last part concerning Phillips) that I played to his parents the next day in a special session in my office. They swore to me that the voice on the tape was *not* Wes's. They said he was a good boy and that what happened to Sister Marcia *had* to have been an accident. I suggested that they allow me to turn Wes over to a children's clinic for an evaluation. I hated the whole deal. They agreed.

I visited Sister Marcia in the hospital. She was overjoyed to hear that Wes was going to be gone for at least a whole week. She then told me that she had never thought she would see the Devil in her lifetime and that she has seen the Devil in his eyes. "He has the eyes of a killer," she said. "Of the Beast." I reminded her that I don't belong to the Catholic Church and that I don't necessarily believe in the Devil. I also mentioned to her that, in any public school, she could NEVER have gotten away with handling a student by the ear like that. (I guess she really didn't get away with it *this* time either though, that's for sure.) "I've been teaching children at that school since before you were born," she said. I told her that it was attitudes like the one she was demonstrating right then that were the reason why so few nuns are qualified to teach at St. Pius Elementary. The school had once been completely staffed by nuns from the nearby St. Ruth Convent. Those days were long gone. But she wouldn't hear it. She cast me out of her hospital room and called me a heathen.

Monday, January 30

I met the Bovas at the hospital and introduced them to the lead psychiatrist there, Dr. William Kanaris. I could tell that, underneath the "good little boy" performance that Wes was maintaining, he totally despised us and his situation. I agreed to be there during the day for his sessions as a representative of St. Pius and an aid to Dr. Kanaris.

Tuesday, January 31

When it was suggested today to the Bovas that Wes undergo hypnosis, Wes lost whatever will to maintain the performance he had left. His parents tried to restrain him, but he slipped free of their grip and made a dash for the exit. His dad scooped him up in his arms but Wes tapped him on the neck and his dad fell to the floor, unconscious. The clinic personnel caught him outside and fitted him with a restraining jacket.

In retrospect, I believe Wes was more than physically capable of injuring his father, but chose not to. He had demonstrated an unusually high level of respect and admiration for his parents and would not, I believe, have hurt either of them for any reason. Wes incapacitated his father by momentarily cutting off the blood supply to his brain by compressing his left jugular vein. When Mr. Bova woke up an hour later, he had a severe headache, but suffered from no permanent ill effects. He was luckier than Sister Marcia.

The following entry is not day-to-day, because I was not allowed to keep my journal with me. This was a mandate handed down by a federal agent who more or less took control of the Wes Bova situation on Wednesday. Dr. Kanaris and myself were to keep the Agent, a man named Cooper, apprised of everything that Wes told us in our interviews and focus groups. Kanaris and I were basically being held prisoner by whatever quasi-government agency our new supervisor hailed from. I suggested to Cooper, who dressed in a dark blue (almost black) business suit, that if we knew what we were looking for, it might be easier to glean the information he was looking for out of him. Cooper agreed and showed us a piece of artwork that Wes had made in art class. It was a pencil sketch of a burglar armed with a machine gun. Cooper told us that it was this picture that brought he and his agency to Wes Bova. Wes had labeled the gun a " G36 Heckler." According to Cooper, such a gun was in the planning stages and he was sent to find out how a seven-year-old boy could render an image of a weapon that was merely in theoretical development.

Cooper ordered that the boy be placed under hypnosis. Wes resisted with everything he had.

He was denied protein and placed in a pitch-black room to sleep in. He was given a hospital gown to wear, one-size-fits-nobody. His dark room had no toilet, merely a bucket. Wes was given roughly two hours of sleep per day. The rest of the time he was kept awake by loud, repetitious music or questioning. All this was ordered by Cooper and it went on for days.

Finally, Cooper called in a specialist. Kanaris and I were allowed to observe from that point on and allowed to contribute nothing. Wes was asked the same questions over and over again. On the third day, he began answering every question with a series of numbers. 917013996. Every question's answer was 917013996. His mother's maiden name was 917013996. He went to school at 917013996. He was born on 917013996. The President was 917013996. His favorite ride at Valley Fair was 917013996. He belonged to the First Church of 917013996. Later, Cooper's assistant informed him that the "399" part of the number sequence was typical of Wisconsin Social Security numbers. Cooper concurred with this opinion and surmised that the number that he was actually saying was 399691701. That social security number, if that was what it was, hadn't been issued to anyone yet, according to records. Wes hadn't been issued his yet. It was late and Cooper told everyone to call it a night.

An hour later, Wes was hauled back into the interrogation room.

After another eight hours of fruitless questioning, Cooper ordered sodium penthanol. Wes gave the same answer (917013996) to the first few questions, but then started to deviate. His answers changed. His mother's maiden name was Storley. He went to school at (he paused) St. Pius. He was born on August 14th, 1973. The President was "George W. Bush." Cooper became irritated by this last answer, said he was resisting, and ordered his specialist to increase the dosage. The specialist then asked him how he drew the gun in his picture. Wes said he did it from memory. The specialist asked from what memory. Wes resisted (which looked like it hurt). Cooper had the dosage upped again, at Kanaris's protest. Wes's little seven-year-old body convulsed and thrashed.

The specialist asked from what memory he was able to draw the gun.

Wes said, straining, "from class."

The specialist asked him what his name was.

Wes said "Senior Chief Wes Bova."

Everybody in attendance had raised eyebrows.

"What branch of service are you in, 'Senior Chief?'" asked the specialist.

Wes's attention was phasing in and out

"Senior Chief, what service are you in?".

"Navy," Wes groaned.

"What unit?" asked the specialist.

More disorientation.

"Senior Chief, where are you stationed? What is your unit's name?"

"SEAL Team... Six."

Cooper professed his outrage and asked his specialist if he was giving Wes water or the truth agent.

"How can you be a Senior Chief in the Navy and be only seven years old?" asked the specialist.

"I'm... thirty-eight" said Wes.

"How can you be thirty-eight and also be seven?" asked the specialist.

The room was silent, except for Wes's gasping breaths.

"How can you be thirty-eight and also be seven?" repeated the specialist.

Eyes closed, Wes said, "Wanted... a... second go... at it all... He promised me... I... would... remember everything..."

"Who promised you?" asked the specialist.

Wes opened his eyes and stared wearily at Cooper and nodded.

"He's resisting, you idiot! Up the dosage again!" Cooper shouted.

The fatal dose of liquid truth was administered.

The Walleye Will Not Return
By Darin Wagner

USS *Walleye* SSN-649
637-class attack submarine
Four days from NAVSUBASE Groton CT, inbound
0216 Eastern Time

Sonar Technician Petty Officer Thomas rolled out of his rack in a groggy stupor and nearly fell through the deck and into the Pump Room. Someone had left the hatch open.

Again.

Adrenalin shot through his body and he pulled himself away from the open hatch before gravity could do its job. He laid next to the open hatch for a few seconds, staring blankly into the darkness of the 22-Man Berthing Compartment, before mustering up the ambition to grab his things and head up to the shower. When he did, he left the hatch open.

There wasn't a line yet, so he proceeded into the Crew's Shower with his rubber shower shoes squeaking against the polished, waxed deck of Middle Level. He went through the open door of the shower room, moved all the way the far bulkhead so the door would clear him, and shut himself inside. He chose the aft shower stall. It was really the only choice. Of the two showers designated for the 95 enlisted crew members, the aft one was slightly wider, permitting him to turn around while inside without difficulty. He took his towel off and got in, shower shoes still squeaking against the deck. The water was, of course, ice cold. It would heat up in a few minutes, but that didn't matter since he was taking a submarine shower. *Turn the water on. Get wet. Turn the water off. Lather up. Turn the water on and rinse off. You're done.* He was almost done with step four when it happened.

The whole boat lurched sharply to the starboard side. Then the collision alarm sounded.

"Fuck!" he grumbled to himself as he quickly rinsed off. He could hear the pounding of a legion of sneakers on the deck outside (merely a foot away from him, on the other side of the bulkhead). Thomas got out of the shower and had to wait for several fully-dressed members of the crew who were already heading up the ladder from 22-Man to their emergency stations. The last of them took the time to stop, turn to Thomas and shout "get dressed and quit standing around!!"

Thomas was at his rack fifteen seconds later just getting his jump suit zipped up when the 1MC squawked to life throughout the compartments. "This is the Captain. The boat has hit something. We're not sure what it was except that it probably wasn't a weapon. Had it been a weapon, we probably would have sustained more obvious damage. So far, it appears we have lost the BQS-14. I want all divisions to check their spaces and give their department heads a full listing of all affected gear and equipment. Carry on."

Thomas headed back to Middle Level and into SES (Sonar Equipment Space) and found that someone was already there and making a quick inspection of the various components that made up the AN\BQQ-5B submarine sonar system.

"Life been interesting?" Thomas asked.

"Very," the other sonarman replied with raised eyebrows. "Broadband heard a buoy being dropped about two thousand yards away from us. Then all hell broke loose. Our depth indications start goin' ape shit an' we start listing to the starboard big time and next thing we know, the BQS-14 doesn't work. Last I heard before heading down here was that we were going to PD anyway, with or without it."

The BQS-14 was a special sonar device set apart from the *Walleye's* primary sonar system. It had originally been designed for under-ice operations and enabled the *Walleye* to more effectively detect ice obstructions in its path. "The 14" was also used whenever the boat went to periscope depth (PD) to further ensure that there were no fishing boats or buoys in the way as the 292-foot-long steel boat made its way upward. It was not a 100 % crucial piece of equipment, but a significant loss nonetheless.

There was nothing wrong in SES. Thomas phoned Sonar with the nearby Dial-X and gave them a report. That verbal report was then sent to the Sonar Leading Chief Petty Officer and from there was repeated to the Sonar Officer who repeated it to the Weapons Officer ("Weps"), who then integrated it into his report to the Commanding Officer.

The 1MC came to life again sometime later. "Let me have your attention, this is the Captain. All reports from all departments have been given to me and based on those reports, I'm going to go ahead and stand down from Flooding and General Emergency. Apparently, the only damage we've sustained was to the BQS-14 and SINS. For those of you who are not qualified in submarines, its the Submarine Inertial Navigation System. Near as we can tell, the damage to the 14 may have been caused by a heavy piece of driftwood hitting the 14's transducer and that's the hunch I'm going to go with at this point. Nothing accounts for SINS's breakdown, but then, nothing usually does. As those in the Nav\Ops department know, SINS is a pretty archaic piece of equipment and is prone to frequent problems. It likes to malfunction at the drop of a hat. Like my wife." There was a pause while the Captain chuckled to himself. Most of the crew remained straight-faced while some shook their heads and joined the chuckle. "There's hardly an underway that goes by where the thing doesn't require heavy maintenance from the Nav\Ops department. Right now, SINS is giving us longitude and latitude that would place us somewhere in central Wyoming. Nav\Ops will probably have it fixed in a few hours, but until then this would be an excellent time for those of you who are working hard on earning your dolphins to take a look at SINS while it's opened up. Just don't get in the ETs' way." The Captain ended his report to the crew by stating that, because of the time of night and an unusually dense fog, visibility through the periscope was next to nothing and hadn't shed any light on what it might have been that caused them damage. The CO then told the crew to carry on.

Sonar

There were three main consoles for the *Walleye's* main sonar system. Broadband. Classification. Workload Share. Each console, or "stack," was manned continuously while the boat was underway, under normal conditions. The three operators were always chaperoned by a Sonar Supervisor ("Soop"). The Broadband operator had to give his stack his undivided attention and was not supposed to talk about anything except what was on his screens. The other two stacks, however, allowed for conversation.

"What the Hell are you smokin'?" asked Class.

"I take it you don't agree with me," said Workload.

"The 80's are going to end with 1989. 1990'll be the first year of the 90's," proclaimed Class.

"No it won't. 1990 is the last year of the decade," counter-proclaimed Workload.

"How can you be so damn *stupid*?"

"I'm not being stupid. I did the math."

"The 80's started at 1980 and will go to 1989. Pretty simple fuckin' math."

"When you count to ten, do you start with zero and go to nine, or do you start with one and go to ten?"

Class paused and then said, "One to ten."

"There you go."

"That doesn't fuckin' *work*."

"Sure it does. The first year of every decade is the one that ends with a one. That's the way our calendar works and has worked since the first year A.D.."

"Which was year zero."

"Nope. There never was a 'year zero' on our calendar. It went from 1 B.C. to 1 A.D.. Which means that the first decade A.D. wasn't over with until the end of the last day of the year 10 A.D.."

"Wait, wait. So what you're tellin' me is that on New Year's Eve 1999, everybody's going to be celebrating the start of the new century one year early?"

Workload nodded.

"Yer fucked in the head."

Workload showed no offense to this and replied, "two thousand years is two thousand years."

"Course, ya know that Christ wasn't really born on January 1st, Year One, right?"

"Doesn't make any difference. The Gregorian Calendar went into effect *retroactively*."

Thomas, who was currently manning Broadband, had heard enough of this argument. It had already gone on for almost an hour. It started out as a simple discussion of "the Greatest Hits of the 70's," but eventually degenerated into the kind of argument that can last for hours upon hours and never be resolved. "The Greatest Hits of the 70's" turned into discussion about when the 70's began/ended and from there to the 80's and then snowballed into full-blown argument concerning the turn of the century. Workload and Class each had a typical "complete-ist" attitude and would never let the other have the last word. Thomas figured they hadn't been around long enough to appreciate the dramatic power of silence.

Thomas *had* to get out of there.

He had been trying to study for his Sonar Supervisor qualification and had his nose buried in his notebook. The notebook was labeled with his full name and rank; STS3\SS Dave Thomas. Someone had taken a pen to the label and scrolled in the words "Founder of Wendy's" under his name. Thomas hated it at first, but then learned to accept the joke. The crew could have thought of a worse moniker, after all. He turned around on his bench and addressed his superior. "Sonar Soop, requesting permission to relieve the fathometer operator."

The Sonar Supervisor looked like he envied him. "You want to relieve him an hour early? Granted."

Control

The Control Room ("Control") was quiet and still rigged-for-dark. Thomas passed by the now disassembled SINS and took note of the sign hanging on it that said "OOC." He politely excused himself as he squeezed past the QMOW (Quartermaster Of the Watch) at the navigation plotting table. He then began his watch turnover with the off-duty sonarman who was still manning the AN\BQN-17 fathometer. The weapons officer had decreed that the fathometer would be manned by each watch for an additional two hours after their watch was officially over. *Why* this was the case was something Thomas could never figure out.

After all the necessary information had been given to him, Thomas turned towards the OOD. He couldn't see the OOD in the darkness, but he nonetheless called out, "Officer Of the Deck, requesting permission to relieve the fathometer operator.

Red Sounding is 1,423 feet.

Yellow Sounding is 1,837 feet.

Expected sounding is 2,866 feet.

Current sounding is 2,230 feet.

Ownship is currently at a depth of 300 feet traveling at all ahead full.

The fathometer is in a non-secure, short pulse mode."

The unseen OOD replied, "Relieve."

"Relieve, aye sir."

After the fathometer log had been properly signed out and in, the former fathometer operator then called out "fathometer watch has been relieved."

The OOD's voice then replied, "Very well."

Control was now quiet again, except for the cooling AFW (Auxiliary Fresh Water) moving through the overhead and into the surrounding electronics in pipes and for the steady, methodical clicking of the fathometer's stylus as it scratched a bottom trace on its chart. The QMOW, who was standing at his plot next to Thomas, looked puzzled.

"What's the matter?" Thomas asked.

"Oh it's nothing, I guess... most of the expected soundings on my charts haven't matched the 17's soundings is all. Can't figure out if I'm using an out-of-date chart or what," the QM replied.

"By how much have they been off?"

"There's an average difference of only about 200 feet. I told the chief and he's sure that these are the most updated charts."

"Could it have been an earthquake? Sonar heard lots of magma displacement earlier..."

"There hasn't been a shift like this in these waters in years, but that's probably it. It's almost like being in the Pacific again."

"Well, it ain't the fathometer. These soundings're pretty solid."

Someone then appeared a few feet away from them. The figure was in a noticeable daze trying to adjust his sight to the darkness in Control. It was the Ensign. He moved past the QM, pushing him uncomfortably against his plotting table.

"'Excuse me' works real well, sir," said the QM in a subdued tone of aggravation as he eased back away from the plot after the officer's passing.

"Oh, sorry... 'scuse me," said the *Walleye's* most junior commissioned officer. Without making eye contact.

The Ensign then turned to Thomas. "So, is the fathometer in an active mode?"

Thomas looked at him and blinked for several seconds. With a straight face, he then replied, "No sir. The fathometer is in a *passive* mode."

"Ah," the nub Ensign nodded.

Thomas's reply was, of course, ridiculous.

The Ensign had newly reported to the *Walleye* two months earlier. He had quickly distinguished himself as being one of the stupidest men onboard and his fathometer question was just one more indication of this. For a man who had done four years of college, passed through the Navy's nuclear power schools (the toughest academic program the military had to offer, no less), and SOBC (Submarine Officer Basic Course), he should have had some semblance of a clue when it came to essential submarine equipment. All fathometers employed active sonar only. They *had* to. That was the only way they could get a sounding. The fathometer sent pulses to the bottom of the ocean and then "listened" for their returns. Based on the speed of sound in the water and the time it took for a pulse to return, the unit would then calculate the distance between ownship and the bottom and spit that information out onto a chart and a digital display. It was the most basic of concepts. (In contrast, passive sonar meant merely listening and not putting any sound in the water.)

"If you're studying for your Junior Officer of the Deck quals, sir," continued Thomas, "the one to ask concerning the BQN-17's passive modes would be the STLPO. He'll hook you up." The STLPO (Sonar Technician Leading Petty Officer) would have riotous time toying with the Ensign on this. The QM was cracking a slight smile while shaking his head.

"Okay, thanks," said the Ensign. He then pushed rudely pushed past the QM again.

"'Excuse me' *still* works, sir."

"Oh, 'Scuse me..." mumbled the Ensign.

Twenty minutes into his fathometer watch, Thomas turned to the QM and asked about SINS.

"Well, the ETs worked on that thing for, like, four hours trying to get it to work right. Each time they put her back together, they got a totally fucked long and lat. And then they got shocked and dropped the last circuit card on the deck. Thing broke in two. So the Captain had it secured. I guess he figured it could stay OOC 'till we get back to Groton," said the QM.

"What else is new?" asked Thomas.

"Nothing, except we're fixin' to secure from Rig-For-Dark here in a few minutes," said the QM. "What's your current sounding?"

"2,000 feet even," said Thomas.

"Damn, that's makes for almost a 600 foot difference from my expected depth." The QM grabbed his calculator and re-verified his information. He didn't look so relaxed anymore.

"Quartermaster, estimated time till sunrise?" asked the OOD, who was looking through periscope number one.

The QM looked at the time display on the bulkhead and then reported, "Sunrise in two minutes, sir."

The OOD turned away from the periscope and addressed the messenger who had come back from the Crew's Mess with a tray of coffee. The OOD grabbed his cup, which had his rank insignia on it (two silver bars) and took a sip. Then he winced. "God dammit, did you put Sweet 'N Low in this?"

The messenger (a nub seaman recruit) just stood there timidly.

The OOD put the coffee cup back on the messenger's tray. "Take this back down to the Mess Decks, dump it all out, brew some fresh stuff and put one sugar, let me say that again, PUT ONE SUGAR in my coffee, stir it and bring it back up here. Never

EVER put that Sweet 'N Low crap in this coffee cup again. Understood?"

The messenger nodded and briskly took off for the Crew's Mess.

"Moron... puttin' that shit in my cup," grumbled the OOD. Then he turned back to the periscope. "Quartermaster, time till sunrise?"

"Sunrise time now, sir," answered the QM.

The OOD peered through the scope. "Quartermaster, verify that sunrise is time now,"

"Sunrise is at 1314 zulu time, sir, which was 25 seconds ago," the QM verified.

"Bullshit, check it again."

"Sir, I've got it right here in front of me. 1314 zulu."

"Well it's just as dark now as it has been for last eight hours, so I *know* your information is off."

"Aye, sir."

All this time, Thomas had been watching his bottom trace and digital display on the fathometer. The fathometer was the first piece of sonar gear that sonarmen on the *Walleye* had to qualify. It was a simple, but extremely important device and it was also one of the most intimidating for beginners. If a boat ever ran aground, the first person that the JAG investigation would go after would be the fathometer operator. The first thing a sonarman learned when he started his fathometer qual card was that, if you didn't do your job while manning it, you were bound for a court martial hearing. The last boat that had run aground was the *Sunfish* and that crew had hated life for years afterward, enduring much scrutiny and observation from not only Squadron Four but also from COMSUBLANT. The fathometer could require more of one's attention and concentration than Broadband at times. Right about the time the messenger had handed the OOD his Sweet 'N Low-tainted coffee, the fathometer's soundings had started to change tempo. Drastically. The numbers were getting smaller at an increasing rate. The current Yellow Sounding was set for 1500 feet. Suddenly, the fathometer read 1479 feet. Thomas let it update for two more seconds to make sure it wasn't a fluke. When it dropped again to 1472 feet he lifted his head and shouted "YELLOW SOUNDING, 1472 FEET!!"

The Control Room party snapped to life and the OOD turned to the Chief Of the Watch at the Ballast Control Panel. "Chief Of the Watch, on the 1MC, Yellow Sounding, All Stop."

"On the 1MC, Yellow Sounding\All Stop, Officer Of the Deck\Chief Of the Watch, aye," repeated the COW as he grabbed the microphone for the 1MC and raised it to his face. "YELLOW SOUNDING\ALL STOP!"

Over the 2MC, Maneuvering answered, "Yellow Sounding, all stop, Control\Maneuvering, aye."

There was a brief moment of silence followed by the Helmsman's report that Maneuvering had answered All Stop.

"YELLOW SOUNDING, 1412 FEET!" continued Thomas.

"What the Hell?!" the OOD said as he forced his way through the cramped Control Room and to the fathometer.

"RED SOUNDING, 1388 FEET!!" reported Thomas. This was now serious. If a boat got a Yellow Sounding, it meant that they had to stop (and submarines don't completely stop once the screw ceased turning). A Red Sounding meant that the risk of running aground was probable, if not imminent, and it meant throwing the screw in reverse.

The OOD told the COW to report "Red sounding, all back emergency"over the 1MC. The COW did as instructed and sounded the collision alarm. Then Maneuvering sent back the acknowledgement and then the report that the screw was now performing backwards.

"RED SOUNDING 1380 FEET!"

"RED SOUNDING 1375 FEET!"

"RED SOUNDING 1368 FEET!"

"RED SOUNDING 1360 FEET!"

"Fathometer operator, shut up!" yelled the OOD.

"RED SOUNDING 1360 FEET!"

"RED SOUNDING 1365 FEET!"

"RED SOUNDING 1369 FEET!"

"RED SOUNDING 1370 FEET!"

"Fathometer operator, I told you to shut up!" yelled the now panicking OOD. "Messenger, go to Sonar and tell them to send a relief for the fathometer operator."

"Officer Of the Deck, *you're* relieved," said the Captain as he entered Control.

"RED SOUNDING 1377 FEET!"

"Yes sir. I stand relieved sir," said the now off-going OOD.

"Fathometer operator, continue to call out red and yellow soundings in accordance with procedure as you have been doing," the Captain calmly said right before taking a slurp of fresh coffee from the cup of the off-going OOD.

"Yes sir. Yellow sounding 1489 feet," said Thomas as he wiped his drops of sweat off of the fathometer's digital display.

"Con/Sonar, we just lost the towed array."

"Sonar/Con, aye," acknowledged the Captain as he grabbed the 2MC and brought it to his set jaw. "Maneuvering, this is the Captain. All stop."

"Yellow sounding 1489 feet."

Maneuvering answered and soon the helmsman reported that the submarine was now completely stopped.

"Quartermaster, based on the soundings that we've had, I want you to re-compute our red and yellows. We're still in well over a thousand feet of water and in no danger of running aground just yet. Do you concur with this opinion, fathometer operator?" asked the Captain.

Thomas was feeling a little better now. "Yes sir, the bottom appears to relatively steady with no sharp depressions or elevations. It's changes are gradual and we should be able to tell well in advance if we get too shallow. But I don't recommend going any faster than a half-bell."

The Captain told Thomas and the QMOW to carry on and then he grabbed the 1MC. "Let me have your attention, this is the Captain. We've run into some inconsistencies between the ocean floor and our charts which lead our fathometer operator to call away both yellow and red soundings. The boat is in no immediate danger of running aground, but this little incident has cost us our towed sonar array, which was severed when the screw went into reverse. That towed array, for those of you who don't know, is going to cost the American tax payers over $10,000 to replace." The Captain paused for a second and looked down at the deck as though he was reading something printed on it. "That is all, carry on."

The Wardroom

Assembled in and the around the green table of the Wardroom was the CO, the XO, all the forward department heads, the radiomen, Thomas and his chief. The officers were sitting at the table, while the enlisted were standing around it behind them. The Wardroom was a multi-purpose space. It usually functioned as the officers' mess, but could also be used as an operating room if the Hospital Corpsman onboard needed to perform emergency surgery. Captain's Masts were held there. It was also the location where confidential meetings took place.

"Captain, as of five minutes ago we still have not heard from Squadron nor have we received any transmissions of any kind since about 0200 zulu," said the Cryptology Officer.

"No radio transmissions? Not even from commercial fishing trawlers?" asked the Captain-in-disbelief.

"No sir," said the Crypto Officer.

"What about radar contacts?"

"None, Captain."

The Captain then turned to the lieutenant whom he had relieved during the red sounding incident. "And still no visual contact of any kind through the scopes?"

"No sir," said the Lt. "It's just as dark out there as it has been since sunset last night."

"And the night vision?"

"With that fog up there, night vision only shows us about five yards of calm water in all directions," answered the Lt.

The Captain sighed and stared at the green table while the assembled remained silent. Then he turned to the Sonar Chief. "How's the bottom, Chief?"

The Sonar Chief stepped forward (with Thomas) as he cleared his throut and placed the fathometer's paper trace on the green table. He turned it so that the Captain and the XO could get a good look. Then the old chief said, "The bottom of the Atlantic three days from Montauk should not look like this. These traces are of a smooth gradient. There should be jagged traces here. But there isn't. And our soundings are still off... by almost 1,000 feet now."

The Captain then looked up at Thomas. "Petty Officer, you've sort of become our fathometer expert after today. Is there anything you'd like to add to the Sonar Chief's statements?" The Captain almost looked like he was pleading for a second.

Thomas spoke up immediately. "Yes, sir. The bottom itself is soft, like sand. What *should* be under us is rock. It should be reflecting the active sonar a little better than this. But this trace is characteristic of the alluvial/granulated floors of the Carribean and the

Pacific. Also, Sonar hasn't heard any biologics in the last eight hours. Except for a very distant one. Sounds like a sick whale."

"Weps, anything to add? Any conclusions?" the Captain said as he turned to his Weapons Officer.

"Yes sir. The state of the ocean floor, as indicated by the fathometer trace, is consistent with," the Weps paused unintentionally, "large scale nuclear bombardment. Earthquakes don't pulverize shale and hundreds of feet of sedimentary rock into fine granules like this. It's just not a natural occurrence. That piece of evidence from the fathometer, added to our inability to detect any radar or radio contacts on any of our antennas, including our IFF and low freq receivers, and the apparent absence of the sun due to an unusually thick and fog-like atmosphere... all of these things, in my opinion, add up to something very big having happened out here. And we just missed it."

The Wardroom was silent for a long moment.

The silence was deafening.

Thomas's Rack

Thomas had been laying in his rack next to the open hatch leading to the Pump Room for over an hour. Minutes after he had delivered his opinions concerning the fathometer trace, the junior enlisted personnel were dismissed from the Wardroom, leaving only the officers and the senior enlisted.

Large scale nuclear bombardment of the ocean floor, he thought. He ran that concept through his head a few dozen times. *Why would anyone waste good nukes on the ocean? If the Russians or the*

*Chinese used some kind of nuclear weapons in the
ocean, what would they gain? What's of value out
here? The SOSUS net? Yeah, that would make sense.
But why not nuke the SOSUS control stations on the
shore? Oh, right...because they're on the shore.
Collateral damage. Yeah... you don't nuke a country
that you want to occupy. Jesus, this is like some
fucked up "Red Dawn" rip-off. So they bomb the net
to prevent us from being able to track any incoming
troop transports or boomers. The loss of any
deployed Navy ships and the loss of a butt-ton of
merchant vessels throws us into defensive and
economic chaos. But there has to be more to it than
this..*

    (The SOSUS net was an impressive array of
hydrophones that spanned the Atlantic. It ran along
the bottom of the ocean and enabled naval tracking
stations ashore to monitor shipping of all kinds,
including loud submarines. It played a valuable part
in the nation's defense.)

    Then Thomas started to think about the
Walleye's unanswered radio calls. *Jesus H. fuckin'
Christ, we're all* alone *out here. We might have to run
aground to get to land. There probably ain't no
Groton anymore.* That thought kept him up for
another two hours along with a few other thoughts.
He thought about his ex-girlfriend, Rose. He thought
about her and her long black hair and her soft lips and
how he might never get the chance to make things up
with her like he wanted to and had planned to. He
thought about his folks in Minnesota and wondered if
they had been incinerated in an atomic flash or if they

were being corralled into a concentration camp somewhere.

Finally, exhaustion took him under.

While he was asleep, he was almost woken up by a commotion above him in Middle Level. Men screamed. Feet raced. He was too tired to wake up then. No alarms went off. But when he did wake up for watch, he found out that the *Walleye* had surfaced and that a diver, one he was friends with, had tried to go topside in his wetsuit and look at the damage done to the 14's transducers. The dosimeters detected no radiation, but as soon as he cracked open the outer hatch of the forward escape trunk, he fell back down into the trunk... dead with a burnt face. He was burnt by whatever the fog was. The men who pulled him out of the trunk were also burned by the residual gas that was still in the trunk.

Four hours after that, the sun decided to come out.

The fog outside the submarine was a deep, rich and unnatural purple color. The Weps looked at it through the scope and, knowing a little something about chemical warfare, proclaimed it as a man-made agent by virtue of its color and by virtue of what it had done to the diver.

All this information was passed on to Thomas while he was at chow. Chow was lasagna but Thomas had a banana and a glass of water.

Sonar

"So, when it comes down to us becoming a bunch'a cannibals, who do ya think'll get eaten first?" asked the Broadband stack operator.

Thomas looked at the guy sitting on Broadband for a second with a cold, deadpan expression and then replied, "Probably the guy we got stuck in the freezer with no face."

"Well, yeah... but I mean, who do you think'll get killed fer their meat first?" asked Broadband with a smirk. "D'ya think rank'll have anything to do with it?"

The Soop spoke up. "If it comes to cannibalism, there won't be much left of our military bearing. But it won't come to that. We'll find our way to a suitable port. Charleston, maybe. If not, we'll set anchor and send boats over to the mainland to look for food and information. But let's talk about something else."

For a while, none of the three men in Sonar said a word. The fourth man on watch was out in control manning the fathometer. As a kind of reward for handling the red sounding situation so well, the Captain told the Soop that he didn't want Thomas to man the fathometer again for a while unless there was another emergency.

"Man... that fucking whale is really close to us now," announced Broadband.

"How close?"

"About 100 yards port side, Soop."

The Soop grabbed his own set of headphones and lined up the sonar system so that he could hear what Broadband heard. "Damn, that's the most miserable whale I've ever heard. He sounds like he's sick or dying or something. Hardly even sounds like a whale. Hey, you know what this reminds me of? Up by Nova Scotia there's this natural whale mating area. Those whales sounded pretty weird up there, too."

"I'd sound pretty miserable too if I were the only living thing in over 2,000 miles," said Thomas. "He's probably sick from nuclear fallout. Or maybe he came up to the surface and got burned just like our boy."

"That would explain the change in tone all right," said Broadband.

The Soop continued with what he was saying. "Anywho, up by Nova Scotia, submarines aren't supposed to enter this whale mating region because it disturbs what their doing. Some of those blue whales are almost as long as us and they've mistaken boats for other whales movin' in on their territory."

Thomas shifted in his chair and looked at the Soop with interest. "Really?"

"Oh yeah. I've read that in whale society, they try to drive sick or injured whales away from the group. And that's what a submarine looks like to them. So they swim along side the boat and try to nudge it and drive it away," the Soop continued. "They can't damage the boats, but they can crack their own skulls open when they ram 'em. And because they're an endangered species, the Navy just tells the submarines to stay away from that area during certain times of the year."

Conversation continued and migrated through subject-to-subject just like it always did in Sonar. The topic eventually shifted to a horror movie that they had seen on the Crew's Mess called "Fright Night" starring Roddy McDowell. It was a vampire flick and from there, the discussion became about Dracula and the novel by Bram Stoker. Thomas was feeling a little better and decided to enter into the conversation by asking a question about said novel, which he knew quite a bit about.

"How does Dracula die at the end of the novel?" Thomas asked with a grin.

"Sunlight," said Broadband.

"A wooden stake," said the Soop.

"Yer both wrong," said Thomas.

"Well, in the movies that's how he usually dies," said the Soop.

"So, how did he die in the book?" asked Broadband.

"He was stabbed in the back by a Texan with a buoy knife," proclaimed Thomas.

"No way," said Broadband.

"That's bullshit," said the Soop.

"There's no way Dracula dies from getting stabbed with an ordinary knife," said Broadband. "That wouldn't kill a vampire."

"Exactly," confirmed Thomas.

"Exactly? What's 'exactly?'" demanded the annoyed Soop.

"Dracula didn't actually die in the novel. He gets stabbed by Quincy and he turns into dust and moonbeams," explained Thomas. "Scholars who've studied the novel and Bram Stoker think that he had planned a sequel novel if Dracula turned into a top-seller. But it didn't sell very good at first, so Stoker never wrote that second book. Later on, of course, the book became a huge hit. But Stoker was dead by then."

"Hey, I hate to interrupt you, *professor*, but our sick friend outside just went quiet," reported Broadband.

"What was the last bearing?"

"About 180 degrees, Soop. About 75 yards away."

"Very well."

Ninety minutes later, the fog seemed to lift somewhat and visibility had improved through the periscope. One could now see almost 100 feet out before the world blurred into a purple haze.

"Soop, our friend is back!" called out Thomas, who now had the Broadband stack. The former Broadband operator was now out in Control manning the fathometer and the former fathometer operator was now manning the Classification stack.

"Something ain't right here..." muttered Thomas.

"What?"

"Flow noise, Soop." Thomas pressed his headphones against his head for better sound. "More flow noise than I've heard in a while. And I never heard a biologic make that much noise movin' through the water. Thought that whale was sick, but he must be really *truckin'*."

The Soop once again put on his headphones and made it so he could hear.

He went pale.

He grabbed his mic.

"Con\Sonar..."

Suddenly, the entire boat jerked to the port side. The noise was unforgettable.

"He rammed us!"

"Damn, I didn't think they could hit us like *that*! Felt like a damn tugboat!" said the Soop as he picked himself up off the floor.

"Sonar/Con: Report!" said the OOD over the squawk box.

The Soop, still shaken up, grabbed the mic again. "Con\Sonar, that whale we've been hearing for the past 24 hours just broadsided us."

Silence on the MC, then, "Sonar/Con, that was a whale?"

"Con/Sonar, y-yes."

"A *whale*?"

"Con/Sonar, yes."

"Sonar/Con, was it in *heat* or what?"

"Con/Sonar, I couldn't tell you."

"Sonar/Con, aye."

"Con/Sonar, judging by the amount of flow noise that it made just before it hit us, I'd say it probably cracked its skull upon impact."

There was another pause. Sonar could hear the OOD discussing something with someone. Then the OOD said, "Sonar/Con, I concur with that opinion. That thing didn't do us any damage, except that one of the cooks had a whole can of lard fall on his ankle while he was in Storeroom Two and one of the electricians back aft shocked himself when the whale hit us."

"Con/Sonar, aye."

"Soop, I can still hear the whale's flow noise," reported Thomas. "It's getting louder again!"

"Sonar/Con. The whale is gonna ram us ag-"

This time the *Walleye* felt like it was both lifted and spun as something the aft section of the port side.

"Mother *fuck*," Thomas said under his breath as he heard the flow noise from the biologic fade away rapidly. He'd never felt anything like that. No one onboard had.

The Captain came over the 1MC and explained as much as he knew about the situation. He said that there was still no significant damage to the boat and the crew. He also said that he was having the boat come to an all stop until further notice.

After two more hours at broadband, an off-duty operator entered Sonar and offered to relieve anyone who needed to go to the head or smoke a cigarette. The Soop told Thomas to go first. Thomas went to the head and then headed to the *Walleye's* "smoke pit." The smoke pit was a few feet aft of Radio and about three feet forward of the watertight door which lead into the reactor tunnel. It was right next to the huge air induction vents that sucked in the ship's atmosphere and drew it through purification filters and scrubbers. It was the only place that the Captain allowed smoking to take place. Other than in his stateroom, of course.

Thomas had just lit his Newport light when one of the radiomen who had been in the Wardroom with him the previous day came by for a smoke. The RM looked beat.

Thomas handed him his lighter. "How goes it?"

"Man, what the fuck was up with that whale?"

"Got me. If it were up to me, I'd go active on his ass at max power and drive him away. But the Captain believes we're at war and wants us to be quiet."

"Well, that thing is fucked up."

"Yeah."

"Hey, if the Captain wants us to be quiet, why are we on the surface?"

"Because that fog out there is something we can't see through. And if we can't see out, chances are pretty good that no one can see in. When it fades away, we'll probably submerge to PD again."

"This isn't good. This really isn't good."

"What?"

"Well, you know that we haven't seen any long range radar contacts or intercepted any radio transmissions, right?"

"Still?"

"Yeah, and that ain't the only thing we ain't got. The Captain has been having us send out for GPS fixes all day in order to find out where we are and what else is out here. We haven't gotten a response back. So now we're sending low freq requests to NAVSAT."

"NAVSAT?"

"Yeah, it's like an older version of GPS. It was pretty much replaced in the seventies. There are still eight NAVSAT satellites in orbit and they use lower frequency transmissions than GPS does. But they're more simple and limited."

Thomas knew how GPS (Global Positioning System) worked. It was a navigational satellite system that could tell a ship at sea, or anyone for that matter, their precise latitude and longitude. It could also take orbital pictures and upload those pictures to the *Walleye*. "How limited is NAVSAT?"

"Very. We send a signal and the sats pick up that signal and automatically aim their camera at the direction the signal came from and take a picture and then transmit that picture back along the same trajectory. Hopefully, back down to us. This fog outside is probably what is preventing us from getting through to GPS. But, like I said, NAVSAT uses lower freq so it might get through." The RM took a drag on his Camel. "There's no guarantee that NAVSAT still works. No one's used it in, like, ten years. And we don't know if the picture we get back will be any help. That fog might cover miles around. The Captain also wants me to get in a steam suit after watch and see if I can set up the Furuno. I'd like to tell him to fuck off."

The Furuno was a standard civilian radar unit that was use by just about half of the yachts and fishing boats in the northern hemisphere. US submarines also had them for when they left and returned to port. The Furuno radars were actually more accurate than the ones built into the sails of US submarines and had much better short-range resolution.

"Where are we supposed to be right now anyway?" asked the radioman as he scratched his crotch.

"The QMOW figured that we should reach Montauk Point in about eight hourse based on current course and speed. But he could be wrong," Thomas said as he blew out another billow of smoke.

"Think it'll still be there?" asked the radioman with a cold look and a soft voice.

"Montauk?"

"No, everything."

"Got me," said Thomas. And then he ground his spent cigarette in the nearby can and went back to Sonar.

Sonar

Thomas came back to find that the Captain had secured the fathometer watch until further notice. But sonar was still to remain in "hot standby" in case the QMOW needed a dedicated operator for it.

Thomas sat down and saw that the Soop was listening intently. Not to what was out in the water, but to what was coming out of the MC. The OOD had left it on and so the Soop was listening to what was being said.

The OOD's voice was a little faint. "Raising number two scope."

The Soop told Thomas to turn up the volume on the speaker.

The OOD came in much louder now. The fact that the sonarmen were, in effect, eavesdropping didn't bother them a bit. They were all voyeurs in a sense.

"Sonar/Con, I just saw a splash about 90 feet off of the starboard bow. Was that our Moby Dick?"

The whole sonar shack winced and covered their ears. Thomas readjusted the volume of the speaker back to its original setting.

The Broadband operator confirmed that the biologic trace was back, though there was no indication that it was moving fast like before. It didn't appear to be aggressive this time and it was making what could almost be considered "happy noises" even though it still sounded like a sick humpback whale.

"Con/Sonar, yes. Our friend is back."

"Very well, I'm going to keep an eye on 'im for a while... see what his problem is," said the OOD.

"Con/Sonar, aye."

The sonarmen all watched for the next half hour as the biologic trace moved around them. It circled them. It went underneath them.

Suddenly, the OOD shouted, "Jesus!"

Over the speaker, it sounded like someone had fallen onto the deck in Control. "Oh shit Oh shit Oh shit Oh shit Oh shit Oh shit Oh shit Oh shit Oh shit Oh shit Oh shit," the OOD's voice trailed. The Diving Officer in Control told the Messenger to go get the OOD a relief. The Chief Of the Watch was next heard over the 1MC saying, "Corpsman, lay to Control."

The Sonarmen continued to listen to what was taking place in Control. That is, except for the Broadband operator, who was fixed upon the biologic trace as it faded quickly from his screen. They could hear the calm voice of the Hospital Corpsman (the "Doc") as he was tending to the now-relieved OOD. The former OOD was having some kind of panic attack, it seemed. What he was saying was hard to make out amongst all the other noise coming through the speaker from Control, but one thing that he did say that Thomas heard loud-and-clear was something that made Thomas forget the dread possibilities that had been in the back of his mind since that meeting in the Wardroom.

What the former OOD had said, what he had *shrieked,* while being looked after by the Doc was, "Whales have *skin*, not scales! Skin!!"

The Crew's Mess

Lunch was fish sticks. Thomas passed.

SES

Thomas sat in the Sonar Equipment Space and wrote a lot of things in his notebook. Lists of his favorite foods. Lists of his favorite comic books and comic book writers and artists. He wrote dirty poetry about skank hookers in Toulon, France who had propositioned him and he wrote beautiful limericks about the beautiful women in Japan who had avoided him because he was an American. He wrote about what he liked about professional wrestling and why he thought it was going to replace the action film someday. He wrote about Rose. He wrote about his old man. He wrote for three hours with his headphones on listening to Falco sing in German.

Then the radioman from the Smoke Pit walked in. Thomas thought he looked like hammered dog shit. "The Furuno's up and running," he exhaled in a hoarse octave.

Thomas turned off his tape player and told him to sit down. There wasn't much room in SES (like the rest of the boat) and the only place to sit was on the floor in-between the components of the massive sonar computer, which took up the whole room.

"I put on a steam suit and climbed out onto the deck," the radioman told him. "The sky's green, th' water is blue and the fog is still purple."

Thomas looked at him with a set of droopy eyes. The radioman's eyes looked like they were going to role up into his head any second.

I climbed up onto the sail and set up the fuckin' Furuno. These things were fallin' into the water. They looked like driftwood. They're floatin'... floatin' all around us."

The radioman was now resting his back heavily on the processor behind him, sprouting sweat. "I stared out into that mist, damn it was hot up there... why's it gotta be so hot?" his lip quivered. "An' I could have sworn I saw another submarine out there. Just like us. A spittin' image of the Walleye, ya' know? I thought I could see another boat out there, just past the fog. With a man on the deck. Dressed in a fuckin' steam suit... jus' like me. Then I blinked and he went away. I had sweat in my eyes and I couldn't wipe it off with the mask on, y'know?"

"Yeah," said Thomas. He was only going to listen to him for a couple more seconds before telling him to see the Doc again. *Heatstroke*, Thomas was thinking. *Hallucinations*.

Jus' before I was done... I saw God, man. He was looking down on me, man... and smiling like we were making him proud. He loves us, man... we fight the good fight, right? He loves us, so why did he fuck us like this? I wanted to ask 'im, but he scared the shit outta me, y'know?"

Thomas never knew the radioman was religious.

"I got down inside the boat and they sprayed CO2 on me to make sure I wasn't still hot. God, it was so fucking hot up there, and then they helped me out of the suit and gave me water and then I went back to Radio."

Thomas reached out to steady him and keep him from tipping over. "I don't think you drank enough water, man. You almost look like you've got heatstroke," said Thomas.

"You don't fuckin' understand, man!!" the radioman rasped. "We're in a goddam fish-bowl, man. God's fish bowl!" He grabbed Thomas's shoulders. "Don'cha see? We're jus' some toy for his fuckin' fish!"

Thomas put his hands over the radionman's. "Listen, I know this whole nuclear war scenario has got everybody scareder'n shit... you're probably like me and haven't eaten anything in two days and that heat up there just made you see things, man. You were just seein' shit."

"No.. No, I was fine. I was fine until I saw this..." the radioman reached into his breast pocket and pulled out a folded piece of paper. "It took long enough, but we finally got a picture back from NAVSAT."

He slowly unfolded the sheet of paper in sweaty hands.

He held it up to Thomas' face, giggling like someone was tickling his sides.

Thomas saw a picture that looked totally black to him. But then he looked at it more closely and recognized the constellation Orion dead center in on the page. In pencil and off to the side were the words "point of signal origin."

End.

Author Darin Wagner is a United States submarine veteran and University of Wisconsin graduate. In addition to writing prose fiction, he is the creator of the superhero graphic novel *Hyper-Actives*, currently available through Amazon.